The Fiending of the Masses

VOTE BOB

A NOVEL BY JAIMEN SHIRES

The Fiending Of The Masses: VOTE BOB

(Book One)

ISBN 978-1541272729 (First Edition, 2018)
ISBN 978-1-7772724-1-8 (Second Edition, 2020)

An excerpt of this book appeared in Datura Literary Journal, France.

All images, layout and design by Jaimen Shires unless otherwise credited.

Printed in Canada
Published by Wharfinger's Press

This book is dedicated to everyone I've ever worked with creatively over the years. Also, those who've inspired me in one way or another to keep going and take on larger challenges within my art and writing.

Thank you.

VOTE BOB

"Great things are not done by impulse,
but by a series of small things brought together."
- Vincent Van Gogh

VOTE BOB

That's how it all started.

Those words, capitalized. Nothing more.

Presented in a bold, white font

evenly spaced, upon a black background.

That's it. That's all it took.

Well, that along with millions of dollars in corporate donations - funneled through marketing departments and lobbyists - to script the simple phrase and brand it across the entire campaign. A phrase made up of merely seven letters, and void of any colour theme. A phrase so simple, it didn't require an added slogan or balancing flavour text.

VOTE BOB

From that point, all it took were years of market research, test panels, meetings and discussions. A multitude of artistic concepts narrowed down, stripped, simplified and edited. Votes of approval and letters of critique from various levels of power within the campaign, and a final stamp of recognition from head office before the design was finalized. Then approved.

It then sat for years more before the time was right. Aging, maturing, biding it's time until the moment was perfect and the environment sufficiently fertile to unleash the marketing juggernaut they had created.

VOTE BOB

It's time was now. It will win, because it can't lose. Every study, virtual test, projection analysis and simulation have proven this. Every variable has been accounted for. Every single minute detail addressed.

This was an idea, materialized with a level of skill and perfection never before seen within its field.

Anyone can have an idea. That's great, the human mind forms ideas all the time. So what?

You must actualize the idea, and then hide its mechanisms within a simple skin.

The perception of simplicity is key.

Key to reaching the majority.

Take an idea, and write it out on paper as thoroughly as you possibly can. Now, take that idea and sum it up into one single paragraph. Next, break that paragraph down – remove fillers and redundancies, needless explanations and details - until the idea can be contained within a single sentence.

Now take that sentence,

and condense it even further

until it can be represented with a simple phrase.

VOTE BOB

Once this has been achieved successfully, the idea is ready to be shared publicly.

That's all it took.

"Hey Joe. Where you goin' with that gun in your hand?"

"This song always reminds me of my buddy, Tom."

"Yeah?"

"Yeah. Me and my friends used to go drink at his place when we were like sixteen, seventeen. His Dad worked late so we would just chill in the kitchen getting hammered and listening to music. Pretty nice place."

"I'm going down to shoot my old lady.
You know I caught her messin' around with another man."

"He a big Jimi Hendrix fan?"

"Not really. Not that I remember. Actually, this song always reminds of a specific night at his place. All the other nights kinda blur together, you know? Anyway, there was this one time his Dad came home and started yelling - he always came home and started yelling - about how his place wasn't a bar for underage punks. Tom would yell back and they would get into it for a while. Family shit, whatever. None of my business. So, usually by this point we'd just pack up and leave - they'd get pretty fuckin' loud and shit, right? - but this time I stuck around, drinking my beer and staying silent while everyone else fucked off. They continued screaming for a bit. Yadda yadda."

"And I gave her the gun.
I shot her."

"So anyway, his Dad finally storms out the door and takes off, too. Then it was just me and Tom chillin'. That's when I remember this song playing while we sat there drinking."

"Makes sense, I guess."

"No, I'm not done. So, like, we're sitting there chilling and he asks me, he goes,'Do you want to know why I invite you guys over to drink here?' so I asked him why, and he goes,'Because after everyone leaves I usually have a fridge full of their leftover beer.'"

"Where you gonna run to now?
Where you gonna go?"

"So, sure enough, he gets up and opens the fridge. He counts nearly a dozen bottles left behind, and brings me back a fresh one from someone else's abandoned box. We sat there until they were done - talking random drunken nonsense that I'll never remember - and then I went home."

"I'm going way down south.
Way down where I can be free."

"And I guess - probably less than an hour later - his Dad came back home. They got back into it, and my buddy put seven holes in him with a kitchen knife."

"Ain't no hangman gonna -
he ain't gonna put a rope around me."

"Haven't talked to him since."

I can't tell if that last part was bullshit or not, but at least the waiter has finally brought over our burgers.

"Hey, Joe. You better run on down. Goodbye, everybody."

"You two need refills?"

We slide over our hollow glasses of melting ice.

Wake up.

No. I don't want to.

You have to.

Why?

You know why.

Yes. I know.

Fine.

Shit.

What time is it?

I need to get a clock for this place or something. I couldn't even give an educated guess as to what hour it may be right now.

Morning? Afternoon? With all these windows thickly draped with blankets it could be any hour at all out there.

Out in the world.

I had to, though. People can't see me living like this.

And I don't want to see people.

Fuck it all.

I need to do something, though.

Feels like I've been laying here for days.

Because you have.

I know.

Time barely penetrates into this cave. The blankets have a bit of a glow between the weave of their fabric. It's definitely day time, and I should definitely take advantage of it.

Yes, you should.

I know. Shut up.

At least I don't have to be anywhere at any specific time.

Maybe that isn't entirely a good thing.

I've heard that it's healthy to have some sort of purpose in one's own life.

I should probably work on that.

Goals, and such.

I have none right now.

I need to get more candles.
Is that considered a goal?

No, it's not.

I know.

Honestly, what I really need to do is find somewhere else to live. Get out of this fucking rut. Seriously. This shit-hole is depressing, but it will do for now. It will have to. I don't have the effort to change anything right now.

My armies are occupied.
Plus, it's free.

Ha, free.

Yeah.

Sometimes free isn't worth it. Showers by candlelight and belly bruises from window sills.

Life is fun.

These candles are pretty good though, and cheap. 'Emergency' candles. You figure with a buzzword like 'emergency' they would cost more.

Scentless. Dripless. Great for emergencies.
Order now and get two for the price of one!

Never even knew there was such a thing, but it beats showering in the dark.

And shitting.
And shaving.

At least I have hot water.

Care of the neighbours, I'm sure.

The Mennonite family living in the front half of this duplex must be unknowingly footing the whole bill.

Mennonites. Damn creepy religion, if you ask me. I've heard some odd stories. The family - with their seven porcelain doll children all clothed in the same dress pattern sewn from the same length of discount fabric - are as stereotypical as they come. I don't even want to imagine what goes on in that house, but that's not my problem. They can run around dressed in seventies motel curtains - with the radio in their pickup truck as the only form of modern entertainment - paying for my hot water.

Completely fine by me.

No.

It's not fine, Reef.

They're living better than you are right now.

Does that make sense?

What're you doing?

Seriously.

You can't keep living here, it's embarrassing.

Look at yourself.

Stop trying to justify this.

I know.

It's just -

At the time I didn't have any choice, but now...

Now there's not much excuse. This is just a situation of laziness, and convenience.

A situation. Not a way to live.

You're right.

I'm right.

I really need to remind myself of that more often. I'm still alive. This might be a comfortable way to die, but I'm not dying.

I'm not dead.

Time to take the blinders off and live again.

This place is a fucking dump. Look at this shit. Clothes, smoke-butts, and hardened candle wax puddles on every flat surface. Not entirely dripless, apparently.

Fuck.

The air in here is so thick and musty. Dust, ash, and skin flakes being inhaled constantly. Gross.

Holy shit, what the fuck am I doing?

Yeah, I need to fix this.

I should get dressed.

Go uptown.

Get candles.

Eat.

Be a human.

Whatever that means.

I wonder if anyone is around.

Of course. Someone will be.

It's a small town. Everyone's around.

True.

Well, not that small at all when you think about it really. It's sprawling outwards into so many suburbs, neighbourhoods and developments lately. There's new corners of this town popping up all the time that I've yet to venture through since they've been rezoned and urbanized.

This town has definitely grown a lot since I was a kid.

Populations do that.

The core is still the core, though.

That's where everything still funnels towards, and that's where I need to go.

Someone will be around.

I need a smoke before I go, though.

But after this smoke, I definitely need to go.

Doesn't matter anymore if I don't want to go.

I need candles.

"What's on your mind, dude?"
"Nothing."

I hate it when people ask me what's on my mind. What type of question is that? The mind is a pizza with a quantum number of toppings. Even if a person understood the question they were asking, they wouldn't have the time for the answer. Nor do I have the time to provide it. Fuck that shit.

If I did, by the time I finished my answer that answer would surely change.

"It's obviously something."
"Never mind. Fuck it. My brain is my burden, not yours."

Picking fries off of my plate while he feigns interest. Not bothered. I'm well into my burger now. Once I move onto my burger I'm done with the fries. Droops knows this.

"Burden me. I don't give a shit."

The words escaped between mashed potatoes, acting like mild silencers from behind his teeth.

I would tell him but the thing is, he doesn't actually want to know. He doesn't really care what's wrong with me, he just wants to know if it in any way affects him. It's fine, I don't blame him for it. Human nature. Self preservation. Whatever.

"Don't worry about it."
"Nah, fuck that shit. What's up, Spudley? Just spit it out."

I hate when people pry. Especially Droops.
What's up? You really want to know what the fuck is up?
Fine.
I'm impatient.
Impatient of a world that sees its own fallacy and futility but

refuses to accept it, and more-so continues to fight against accepting it.

I'm intolerant.

Intolerant of a system that forces me to function in a way that isn't logical or efficient.

And it's made me insensitive.

Insensitive towards my surroundings, because I don't want to be here. I don't understand the rules. Well, I understand the rules but they're inherently flawed and everyone seems to ignore this blatantly obvious detail. So, I try to maintain a level of numbness in order to cope with the everyday but now and then my thoughts begin racing out of control and all efforts to calm them down steer focus away from other aspects of my self-control, allowing for a little bit of emotion to seep through.

But actually, at the moment I still can't stop thinking of the night before, and the weight I'm still carrying from it.

The panic. The confusion.

The long, long night behind me now.

Thank God.

My brain is tired.

But I can't help feeling that sitting here in this burger joint with Droops is a big waste of my time right now,

"It's nothing."

"It's fucking something. You just paused before speaking and stared into nothingness for like thirty fucking seconds. Total 'Wonder Years' style. You played out a fucking monologue in your head, dude. Just say it. What's up?"

It's the universe, it's the piece of potato stuck to your lip, and it's everything in between.

"It's nothing."

It's everything.

"Just fucking tell me dude."

"Just fucking tell you, eh? I don't really know what it is you want to hear. I'd tell you, but you wouldn't listen properly. Fuck. Put it this way, think of an apple. Picture an apple in your fucking head."

"Okay. Calm down. Sure. I'll picture an apple in my fucking head."

"So, what colour was your apple?"

"Red."

"Mine was green."

"So?"

"Exactly. There's no point in trying to explain. It's like oil and water."

That should shut him up. I can see him thinking about it. Holding a fry.

"So am I the oil or the water?"

"What the fuck does that matter? Be whichever one you want."

"Well, I'm the red one."

"Yeah, and I'm the fucking green one."

"Suit yourself."

"I usually fuckin' do."

"Whatever."

"Yup, exactly. I'm glad we had this talk. It was fuckin' therapeutic."

"Indeed."

Fucking Droops.

Fuck this. I need a smoke.

"I'm going to just pay up and go for a smoke. See you outside."

He reaches for more fries.

"Hey you fuckin' fuck. Dick suckin' fucktard piece of shit. Fuckwad. Cheese dick. Fuckin' piece of shit faggot cheese dick fucktard."

"Yup. Mornin'."

"Give me a fuckin' smoke, you fuckin' piece of shit."

That's how Granger woke up in the morning.

Stumbling out of his room to greet whoever was present with a childish barrage of simple swear words.

Usually just me. It didn't bother me, though. I was used to it by now and his words were generally harmless gibberish. When he was like this it usually meant he was in a good mood, actually. He's talking, and starting the day with a cigarette rather than being up all night on PCP and hard liquor - or whatever the hell a psycho like him functions on – and this is a good thing.

"And give me your fuckin' light, too. Fuckface. So what the fuck is up?"

"Not much."

Why did I move in with this guy?

Granger. The grungiest stranger one might ever meet. He reminded me of a young Bobby Liebling - from the band Pentagram - but with a face from his later years.

Like, seriously.

Granger kind of looked like a foot.

"Meet Granger. Granger The Stranger.
Granger The Stranger's not strange, he's stranger."

We don't talk much. Just smoke and drink together while I act as a speed bag for his swear words. Could be worse.

Frankly, when I moved in here I figured it would only be a month or two before he ended up back in jail and I could keep this place as my own. Granger doesn't usually get too long of a vacation on the outside before he finds himself back home behind bars. From what I've heard. Six months now, and he's still a free man. For now. His hair's grown quite a bit since rolling with the skinheads on the inside, actually.

Never thought about it until now.

What a fucking waste of flesh.

Cheap rent, though.

Hmmm. What the -

That big green dufflebag wasn't there when I went to bed last night. I don't like it. What is it? I know better - I know enough to know that I shouldn't ask what's in it - but I can't help myself,

"What's in the bag?"

"This bag? Ha. Check this shit out, fucker. It's a cement saw. Picked it up last night."

Wonderful.

"Oh, yay. I'm guessing I shouldn't ask where you got it?"

"Probably not."

"Fair enough."

"Throw down some weed. I'll chop it up."

"With that? Yeah, that'll never work. Anyway, I'm all out."

"Well, just grab an eighth from the freezer and spin some up."

Right.

That was the other reason I live here. Weed on tap, or at least in cheap and steady supply. Granger's a shitty dealer - quite possibly the worst - but the weed's good. Granted, it's still arguable if the whole situation is worth it.

"Want to see what this saw can do?"

"Fuck man, I'd rather not. Not in here."

"Pffft. Fuckin' pussy. Either way I'm going to have to take this thing for a spin before I try and sell it. Gotta make sure it works."

"Yeah, well, not much concrete in here."

"Yeah, well -"

I can see his eyes scanning the room for a suitable replacement.

They briefly stop on me.

Eyes sunk deep into the balls of his ugly foot-face.

"Don't even think about you fucking psycho."

"Then hurry up and roll a joint, fucknuts."

"So what's the plan?"

"The plan? The plan was to come here and eat a burger. Which we did."

"Yeah, and now what? Give me a smoke."

"What's with you and fucking plans? There's no plan. Now what? Now nothing. Here's a smoke."

Awkward silence.

Time passes.

Just standing there.

Smoking.

Looking past each other and around each other without making direct eye contact. Thinking thoughts in our own heads with no intention of sharing. Just staring outwards at this stupid fucking town, and saying nothing.

Everything about this area is too familiar.

Everything.

We ate burgers here at least three times a week. Why?

Well, we're creatures of habit, I suppose. This place is also dirt cheap, has free refills, and for lack of a better term we were all essentially 'takeout junkies'.

I can't remember the last meal I cooked.

Hotdogs, I think.

Well, the last *real* meal I cooked.

Frozen pizza? Mac and cheese? Peanut butter sandwich?

It was probably pasta.

Even then, just some simple spaghetti noodles and a can of no-name sauce heated up separately then poured on top.

Bulk parmesan sprinkled generously across the plate.

With some toasted Wonderbread.

Buttered.

It was disappointing, and definitely not a real meal.

I'm a fucking lazy chef, though.

Don't really see the point in all the effort.

A lot of work just to save a couple bucks. Not only am I usually disappointed afterward, but then there's the remorse of the cleanup. An assortment of dishes that will now soak for days in the sink. Not to mention the realization that you made way more pasta than you could possibly eat, so now you're faced with the dilemma of throwing it out or putting it a container to slowly mold and transform in the fridge. Every action has a reaction, so sometimes I find it's best to just limit the actions.

Then there's the moment during digestion where your body realizes that although the meal was heavy and filling, it contained no meat. No protein. I think the effort – no, experience - of cooking for one is why people like me rarely cook for themselves. Very little satisfaction involved.

Much easier when you're cooking for a few people, or at least someone else besides yourself.

"I wonder if anyone's around."

"Huh? Oh. Well, fuck. We could go for a walk, I guess. See

who's at the park, or the coffee shop."

"I suppose. Doubt anyone will be there, though."

"Fine. I don't know, man. What do you want to do?"

"Well, I guess we need some sort of plan. Can't just stand here all day."

"Why the fuck do we always need a plan? There's no plan. Let's just find the closest place to sit, and then sit. Then we're not standing. Is that enough of a plan for you?"

Fucking Spudley and his fucking plans.

"Sure."

"Unless you have a better plan?"

He doesn't. I can see that he wishes he did, but he doesn't.

"Sitting is fine."

That's right. I win.

This is boring.

Sitting sucks.

"Odd."

"What?"

"Well, I was just thinking. Have you seen all these hate ads and propaganda against the different parties during this election?"

"Yeah, how can you not? It's fucking everywhere lately. So what? Same shit that always happens, it's just the way elections go. No big deal."

"Yeah, but then there's this Bob guy. His angle is completely different. With him there's nothing. I mean, I've seen all sorts of commercials and bus ads and crap all over saying don't vote for this guy or that guy, or this person is evil and that guy is corrupt but this Bob guy - well, I don't think I've seen a single attack ad against him. Whether it be from another party or independently. Just these weird and ominous 'VOTE BOB' signs."

"Okay, sure. So what's your point?"

"My point is that it's odd, don't you think?"

"I don't know, man. I guess so? Everything is odd if you really think about it."

"Whatever. I need to go get smokes."

"Alright, whatever. I'll just chill here and man the fort. Guard this sweet bench. Prime sitting spot."

"You do that."

I will.

"Us mortals have finally earned ourselves another halo. After more than five years since the critically-acclaimed album 'The Downward Spiral', Trent Reznor's Nine Inch Nails have officially released their full-length follow-up, humbly titled 'The Fragile'.

The Fragile is recognized as the third studio album from the group, but is more affectionately listed as Halo 14 within their eclectic discography, riddled with singles and stop-gap releases.

Those expecting an angst-ridden follow-up to TDS might be initially surprised by the sound displayed on this double-disc affair, but in time will find - as I have - the natural progression and maturity displayed throughout the compositions. It's definitely an album that grows on you. Each listen seemingly peeling back new layers of bubble-wrap revealing lush and honest compositions across the 'Right' and 'Left' discs, as they are simply named.

Although the previous album boasts hits like 'Closer', 'Hurt', and 'March Of The Pigs' - which all received heavy rotations - the depth of sound within the less angsty singles from this release will surely be looked back upon as a demonstration of a more mature Reznor. One that is aging like a fine wine...blah, blah, blah."

I've seriously read these magazines too many times, and this is even one of the newer ones. Need to get some more material in here. Seriously. It's shit like this - or shits like these I suppose - that cause Alzheimer's. Repetition.

Hurry up, shit.

I swear, as I keep getting older it takes longer and longer to take a dump. Probably not a good thing.

My body is more than likely falling apart inside.

Oh well, fuck it.

Putterputterputterputter..........PUTTERputterputterputterputter

What the fuck is that sound?

Wait. No. Granger better not be trying to -

PUTTERPUTTERPUTTERvrrrnnngggVRRRNNGGvrrnggVRRNNGG

Oh, fuck no. This isn't good.

VVVVVVVVRRRRRRRRRRNNNNNNNGGGGGGGGGGG

Throw the magazine back on the pile,
pinch the turd and wipe up.
Quickly.

VVVVVVVVRRRRRRRRRRNNNNNNNGGGGGGGGGGG

Fuck, it's hot outside.

What were you expecting?

I don't know. I guess from within my blanket fort it's hard to gauge the weather outside. It's October. I figured it would be gloomy. Overcast. Grey.

It's not.

The trees are vibrant with colour. Rusty hues between fiery bursts of red and orange.

It's nice.

This is one of those days where kids' jackets rest in a pile in the schoolyard while their owners run around and play without them. Kicking leaves, and diving into hand-built piles..

Explosions of dead leaves.

I needed this fresh air.

Really needed this.

But this sun, though.

Not used to things being this bright.

Being cooped up in a dark home for days with blocked windows makes too it easy to forget the outside world.

Hiss at the light and crawl back into the shadows.

But I need smokes.

And food.

And candles. Don't forget the candles.

So bright.

Suck it up, Buttercup.

I suppose I could use some sun though. Vitamin D.

My body craves the D.

Weird that sunlight is so important to the human body.

I remember reading about a guy in India who could just stare at the sun without blinking for a solid hour each day, and because of it didn't need to eat any food. Personally, I call bullshit. He must be eating something. That can't be healthy. Someone's sneaking him peanut butter sandwiches in the middle of the night when no one is watching.

You can't just live off the D.

Like some sort of sun slut.

Just craving the D, and nothing else.

Stupid Droops and his sexual innuendo. He's gotten to me.

Vitamin D has been forever spoiled.

It's dirty and raunchy now.

Just like Droops.

Fuckin' Droops. I miss that guy.

But yeah, whatever.

I'm craving the D right now.

Tilting my head back and letting the D splash across my face.

Who gives a fuck?

It feels good.

Oh man, the weird crap that runs through a person's head when they're all alone. I hope there's someone around to talk to when I get up town, I think I'm also a bit lacking in human contact.

Just a little.

You think?

Whatever.

I haven't seen anyone in a while. So what?

I should do something about that.

I know.

Maybe Droops will be uptown

Maybe he's craving the D, too.

Stop. Focus.

Right. Smokes. Food.

And candles.

VVVRRRRNNNGGG VVVRRRNNGG VVRRNG VVRNG

"What the fuck dude! Stop! Shut it off!"

VVVRRNGG VVVVVVVVVRRRRRRRRRNNNGGGGGG

"What the fuck are you doing? Fuck! Stop!"

The blade slices cleanly through a wooden chair.

"HAHAHAHAHA! THIS THING IS GREAT!"
"STOP! Fuck, shut the thing off man, fuck!"

VVVVRRRRNNNG VVVVVVRRRRRRRNNNNGGGGGGG

Another clean slice, through the chair and into the floor beneath.

"YEEEEEEESSSSSSSSS! HAHAHAHAHAAHAHAHA"
"NOOOOOOOOOOOO! FUCK DUDE! STOP!"
VVVRRRNNNG VVVRRRNNNGGGG
"STOP! SHUT IT OFF!"
VVVRRRNNNGGGGGGG
"HAHAHAHAHA"
"STOP!"

I have to stop him.
No, just let him do his thing. This is what you want.
This sort of shit will write its own ending.
Let it happen.

Fog doesn't listen to the wind.
Nor does it argue.
It just waits for it to leave.

Patience.

This problem will fix itself.
You've known this from the beginning.

Patience.

Breathe.

...the smoke is thick, though.

"You buy two pack. Cheepa."
"No, that's okay. I only want the one."

Every single time I come in here this little Asian guy behind the counter says that same thing, and every time I refuse.

You figure he would learn by now.

Or, I guess maybe he figures I would be the one to learn by now. Whatever.

It's definitely more cost efficient to buy the two packs at once. It's basic math, but I just can't justify spending that much at one time on tobacco.

Doesn't work with my daily budget.

It'll put me over.

But I guess my daily budget concept doesn't work well with how the world functions.

Bulk is always cheaper.

Obviously.

Spend more to save more.

But I don't want to spend more.

I feel like I'm forgetting something.

Think.

Right.

TP.

...for my bunghole.

"Oh wait. Hold on one second. I need to grab some TP."

Snatch up a couple single rolls.

Another thing I should probably know better about now.

Buying rolls at a buck a piece from the Asian corner store may be cheaper at the moment, but far from it in reality.

They're buying twenty-four packs for ten bucks, breaking them open, wrapping a piece of tissue paper around the fuckers, and making decent profit.

Fuck it.

I also don't feel comfortable spending a lot of money on shit-tickets at one time. I should at least get three rolls, though.

Buying rolls for a buck - like I would pop or chips - just makes more sense to me.

Pop.

Good idea. I should grab a pop.

Ha, shit. Another thing where they're breaking open a two-four in order to make crazy profit.

A bulk mentality - mixed with Western laziness - can make for decent turnaround I suppose.

Indeed, it does.

"Hey, Reef! How's it going?"

What the- Who? Oh, shit it's-

"Spudley! Hey, man. Good to see you. It's going, you know. Same old shit pretty much."

"Cool, man. Hey, I heard about what happened, if there's any-"

"Nah. It's all good. I'd rather not talk about it."

"Alright, man. That's cool."

Fuck, I haven't seen Spudley in a while.

Right, I keep forgetting I haven't seen *anyone* in a while.

Kind of been hiding in my cave of solitude. I should get out more, some human contact would probably do me good.

Yeah.
Yeah, it really would.

I suppose I should see what he's up to.

Fuck, I should see what Reef's up to right now. He'd probably be a good person to explain my situation to. I know he's been going through a lot lately but I'm sure he'd know of a way to help.

Better than Droops.

Fuck Droops.

"Well, what're you up to?"

"Just grabbin' some essentials. Smokes n' shit tickets. You?"

"Yeah I need smokes. You want to go blaze one or something? Got your car here? Go for a cruise?"

"Walked here, but I'm down to chill and have a toke. Just let me pay for my shit."

"Cool. No worries, I'll meet you outside."

Yeah, I can tell Reef.

He's actually the perfect person to tell. He might be the best person to help me right now, while maintaining secrecy. I know and trust him well enough, and although I know Droops better I think I would trust Reef more.

All I know is, I can't keep walking around uptown like this.

In public.

I need to go somewhere, sit down, and take a bit of this weight off my shoulders.

Or crotch, I suppose.

Even if it's just for a moment.

This has already been a long day.

Here he comes.

"Alright, man. I'm good."
"Cool shit. Where do you want to go?"

A strange pause as we both just stand there thinking about it for a moment.

It's weird when you get older and you're still seeking out places to comfortably smoke a joint. I can see him looking off into the distance, thinking about a good spot. Stripping the duty free tape from around his smoke pack, opening it up, pulling one out and lighting it with a Bic ready and waiting in his palm. Still thinking.

Reef's been through a lot lately. I've got time to give him.

To let him think.

The graveyard's the closest spot, but definitely not appropriate.

He turns and looks the other way.

Smoking.

I wonder what's going through his head right now.

Some of his thoughts become words...

"You know what? Fuck it. Let's go to where I'm staying. It's just down the street."

"Alright, works for me. Where you staying at?"

"Long story, but no one's there. Oh, and we have to climb through a window."

I like long stories that involve climbing through windows.

"Cool shit. Lead the way."

Where the fuck is Spudley?

He should have been back by now.

Left me just sitting here like a loser on this 'VOTE BOB' bench.

Out of smokes.

Fucker.

Vote Bob. Fuck that.

I guess this election thing is coming up pretty quick.

Tomorrow, I think? The day after, maybe?

Good.

It'll be nice to not be reminded about it everywhere I go.

Sick of all these signs.

Even though I won't vote, I kinda hope this Bob guy wins with his cryptic campaign.

It's dark.

I like it.

But it is odd, I guess. Spudley's right. Nobody seems to know anything about this guy.

'VOTE BOB'

That's all the signs say, but I guess it's all they need to say, really. Just a bold, black and white statement - like an explicit warning label - right to the point. No fucking pussy-footing around the bullshit tree. Kind of makes voting for Bob something I could see myself doing.

Even though I don't vote.

And I won't.

But it seems right, because it somehow feels wrong. Bob is obviously who you shouldn't vote for and that's part of the appeal, I guess. The intrigue. This idea of potentially going against the grain but within the system. Like taking door number three, when you know you should probably stick with the prize you've already got.

At least that's what I see.

I like Bob, though. Whoever the fuck he is.

Maybe that's the whole thing. This mystery that surrounds 'Bob'. No one knows who the fuck he is, and as far as anyone knows for certain, there may be no Bob at all. He's as alive as

Schrodinger's cat, and we aren't allowed to open the box.

Not until after the election, at least.

The 'Vote Bob' signs sprouted up all at once it seems. In a single instant one morning after a heavy rainfall, like mushrooms. The other candidates popped up more gradually - seeding and taking root, expanding – but Bob's entrance was much different.

So sudden and absolute. Strange.

I remember when I noticed them. The signs. You could find them sprinkled across lawns - sure - but they were also in the middle of round-a-bouts and bushy medians between road lanes. Creating fairy circles around the perimeters of fences where grass grew to an older age by clinging to the links. They even pushed up pavement to take root in places roots shouldn't be.

Bob's like a weed - one that can seemingly grow anywhere - but a weed that's still oddly ornamental, and visually fascinating for the way it contrasts its surroundings.

Some people had even taken to clipping specimens and displaying them prominently in public facing windows.

You can't really go anywhere without being reminded of him, really.

Not lately.

The Bob signs stand out because they just seem more honest, if that makes any sense. They know they aren't pretty. They know that they aren't colourful. They're man-made. They didn't grow from seed or spore and they didn't feed off of sunlight and water. They aren't natural, and they don't pretend to be.

They're closer to aquarium decorations.

It's enough to fool the fish, though.

Plus, elections themselves aren't really natural either.

Maybe Bob is making light of that fact.

But.

If I think more about it.

It's one of the few things Bob isn't hiding.

This whole situation is extremely veiled.

Who is Bob?

Meh.

Fuck it. Who cares?

What does it matter?

What fucking difference will it make?

Trying to contemplate whether this is the guy I want to lead me is like picking an employer. I never wanted the job to begin with. Besides, nobody really knows what they want.

Just as nobody really knows what they don't want.

Bob wasted no time trying to convince anyone otherwise. He wasted no time doing anything at all.

Bob's job isn't to convince anybody of anything, though. It's simply to be voted for. I guess it's easy to stand behind something that makes no claims to stand for anything. It opens the imagination to anything you might want to believe it could stand for. Since Bob claims nothing he's possible of anything. Faced with the predictable political choices, a gamble with this Bob guy almost seems logical.

Almost.

Fuck. This Bob guy may actually win.

Where the hell is Spudley?

puh-put-putter-putter-puh-puh-put-putter-putter-put-puh-put

That was fucking fun. Time to get high.

"Shit, that was fucking fun. Let's get high. Roll up another joint, fuckhead."

"Fuck dude, you're a fucking psycho!"

puh-put-putter-putter-puh-puh-put-putter-putter-put-puh-put

I'm a fucking psycho? Fuck this guy.

Puh-put-putter-putter-puh-puh-put-putter-putter-put-puh-put

"I'm a fucking psycho? Fuck you! Roll up a fucking joint before I test this bitch on bone."

puh-put-putter-putter-puh-puh-put-putter-putter-put-puh-put

I bet this thing would cut through bone like butter.

Puh-put-putter-putter-puh-puh-put-putter-putter-put-puh-put

"I bet this thing would cut through your fucking bones like butter."

"Whatever, can we at least go outside to smoke a fucking joint? It smells like a dirt bike's been doing donuts in here. That saw spits out a lot of smoke, dude."

"Look what it did to that fucking chair!"

"Yes, I can see what it fucking did. You're fucking crazy, and I'm sure the upstairs neighbour is calling the cops right now."

puh-put-putter-putter-puh-puh-put-putter-putter-put-puh-put

Fuck that stupid bitch upstairs.

Puh-put-putter-putter-puh-puh-put-putter-putter-put-puh-put

"Fuck that stupid bitch upstairs. I'll chop her up, too. Maybe I should cut a hole up through the floor, right into her living room."

"Maybe you should calm the fuck down for a little while, man."

"Just roll the fucking joint, bitch."

"Whatever. Just put the saw down for a bit."

puh-put-putter-putter-puh-puh-put-putter-putter-put-puh-put

Yeah, make me. Fucker.

Puh-put-putter-putter-puh-puh-put-putter-putter-put-puh-put

"Make me, fucker."
"Fuck, dude! Stop!"

puh-put-putter-putter-puh-puh-put-putter-putter-put-puh-put

I'll stop.
Right after I take a little chunk off the end of this coffee table here...

VVVRRNGG VVVVVVVVVRRRRRRRRRNNNGGGGGGG

"So, yeah. Ummmm. We need to hop in through the window."
"What? Why? Just let me in through the front door once you're inside."
"Wish I could. For some stupid reason it needs a key from both sides."
"Weird."
"Not weird, shitty. Just climb in."
"This still seems kind of fucked up."
"Don't think about it, dude. Just do it."
"Well, give me a boost at least?"
"Fuck, what are you, a girl? Just climb in the window."
"But those weird kids are staring at me."

"Ignore 'em, or stare back, I don't fucking care."

A row of porcelain children watching silently as I reach for the window frame. Their fragile, polished faces don't even blink. Like statues. That's fucking creepy.

They're just staring.

If you stare back they stare harder.

Stop it. Stop looking at me.

Weird 'Village of the Damned' type shit. I'm waiting for those blue eyes to start glowing.

Stop it.

Stop.

I bet these weird kids probably sleep with their eyes open. Slightly illuminated throughout the darkest fucking hours. Just this mechanical blue glow across their bedrooms. Cold and unwavering. Their own creepy night lights.

Stop it. Stop looking at me.

"Climb in! Fuck dude, don't worry about the little Mennonites. They won't do anything."

They didn't have to do anything.

Fuck.

That collective stare will haunt my dreams.

If you stare into the abyss, the abyss will stare back.

Oh, it's staring.

How do I wash this feeling off of me?

Just blink.

Once.

One of you.

Please.

"Go! Fuck!"
"Okay, sorry."

Snap out of it.

Can't remember the last time I had to crawl through a fucking window. Even with the invitation, it doesn't feel right.

Infiltration.

I still feel like those fucking kids put a curse on me.

The thought of their collective gaze against my back gave me the final push I needed to breach the threshold, and I'm left blind after the change of settings..

My pupils need to adjust.

"Yo."
"Umm, yo?"

Huh? What the fuck? Hey? Wonder what these guys want.

Hold your pose. Show no fear.

Awkward pause.

Prolonged glare.

"Come over here."
"What's up?"
"Just come here for a minute."

Do I?

Not much option, really.

Fine, I'll walk over. Walking.

Okay, now what?

It's never good when a car full of Asian gangsters roll up and ask you to 'just come here for a minute'.

Nah, tell me what's up first.

"What's up?"
"Just come here."

I'm close enough to talk.

They want me closer.

Fuck.

Did I do anything? I don't think so. Stand here and hold my ground, or walk right up to the car?

Oh well, whatever.

Walking.

Let's just figure this out.

"Alright, what's up?"
"Where's your boy, Spudley?"
"Spudley? Haven't seen 'im."
"No?"
"Nope."
"Alright, well -"

He's eying me up but that's all he's going to get from me.

Stay composed.

Spudley?

Hmmmm.

Wonder what Spudley did.

"If you see him tell him we're looking for him."
"Alright, will do."

Spudley's got business with the Asians? Wonder if that's why he bolted this morning, and why he was acting so weird.

Whatever, not my fucking problem.

Fuckin' Spudley.

Guess there's no sense sitting around waiting for him anymore. Fucking guy.

Well, fuck.

Now what?

I should maybe head out to Bob's, grab some green.

Yeah.

I could definitely go for a toke.

Too much sun out here today anyway.

Go have a toke in the dank basement.

Yeah.

I hope he's home, I don't really like dealing with his psycho roommate.

Fuckin' Granger.

Light calibration complete.
Adjusting focus.
Vision restored.
Analyzing...

Fuck, Reef.

This place is a fucking dump.

No wonder I've never been over before. Ever.

This is how you live?

Clothes crumpled and strewn around across the room over and under piles of mottled clutter. Styrofoam containers and pizza boxes building tilted cities upon a shaky foundations. Coffee table overflowing with beer cans, smoke butts, condiment skins, candles, and just the general squalor you would find in your average everyday heroin den.

I'm confused though. Reef has money. Reef has a car even.

And he doesn't do anything hard,

as far as I know.

"How the fuck do you live like this, Reef?"

"Judge. Go ahead. Whatever. I really don't give a fuck. It's a dump. I know. I'm working on it."

"Yeah bu-"

"Can we just smoke a joint? I didn't invite you over to get lectured. Not in the mood."

He grabs a seat on the couch. Obviously the same spot he always sits at, in the eye of the storm that is his coffee table.

Fuck, Reef. This is bad.

My eyes and mind keep scanning across all the debris in the house, trying to catalog it all. Something about this place being Reef's didn't add up. Nothing here looked like it was his, except for a couple isolated islands of clothes and the shrapnel on the table.

"So, yeah. This isn't my place."

Right. Obviously.

"What?"

"This isn't my place. In case you were wondering. Remember Jodi?"

Yeah, I think I remember her.

"Jodi? Nope."

"Lesbian chick? Four nipples? No? Well, anyway I used to come drink here with her. She's living with some chick now milking her for all she's worth. Skipped on rent and bills, and just left the place like this."

"So she lets you live here?"

"Yeah. Sort of."

'Sort of' means no.

"I'm sure she'll let me the next time I see her, and I'll be out of here by the end of the month. I just keep this nice fatty rolled on the table for if she walks in."

Now things are making more sense. Somewhat.

Still, Reef doesn't need to live like this.

The whole place is dark and dank and the light that barely shines through the edges of blankets covering windows leaves a beam of glittering dust across the room.

Dust has a high percentage of human skin.

I'm breathing in Reef's skin.

And the old, stale skin of a four-nippled lesbian.

Gross.

"Mind if I crack a couple more windows?"

"Go for it."

The breeze billows in through the pillars of light, diluting the airborne flakes. The skin pours into the outside air as an invisible cloud of mixed DNA.

So gross.

Try not to think about the skin.

Move on.

Roll some weed.

There's barely any room on the table to roll a joint comfortably. Any patch of surface I wipe my palm over reveals itself to be covered in dried wax and ash. I blacken the outside of my hand in order to clear enough space to hippie rip a bud.

Roughing it.

"You still haven't told me what happened, Spudley."

"Yeah, I know. I'm building up to it, just let me get this joint rolled. It's been a long night."

What I really need is sleep, but I can't sleep until I'm comfortable. Still some weight that needs to be dropped.
Not the most ideal of settings.
Used to a bit more comfort.
Oh well.
At least I'm safe here, and safety is almost like comfort.

Almost.

"Is there a fire? Why does it smell like there's a fire burning down here?"
"Sorry, Mrs. Mancini. No there's no fire, we were jus-"
"Well, my smoke alarm went off and it gave my heart the biggest jump and I could smell the smoke and I just worry about all my little babies an-"
"It's okay Mrs. Mancini. Your cats are fine. There's no fire. You don't have anything to worry about just go back upstairs, it was just a-"
"Well, I was just so scared and worried because the beeping was going and I could smell the smoke and are you sure they wasn't a fire down here becau- "

Oh. My. God. Bitch.
Shut the fuck up.
There's no fire. Crisis averted. The smoke alarm has stopped.
The cement saw is packed up.
Why are you still talking?
Fuck.

I can just picture her stupid mind making conversations out of the most trivial events...

'And so I couldn't find my sock, and I was certain I just had it, but it wasn't there, and so I went and looked in the bathroom because that was the last place I remembered it being but my sock wasn't there either. So then I figured one of the cats took my sock, because Marshmallow likes playing with socks, but Marshmallow was sleeping on the fuzzy toilet seat cover so he couldn't have taken my sock, but I couldn't find it anywhere'

...Ah fuck, why am I imagining dialogue in my head which is probably worse than what she's actually saying.

"- and I'm really worried about fires happening because there was this one ti-"

She's still fucking talking. Is it rude to just shut the door? Can I just smile and wave at her and say, 'Goodbye' and then as politely as possible just close the door in her face while she's still talking?

"Is that bitch still going off about the smoke alarm? It stopped. Tell her to shut the fuck up before I chop her up into bite-sized pieces. Fuck!"

"Excuse me? What did he just say?"

"He didn't mean it Mrs. Mancini – ummm - he's drunk."

"Even if I were drunk, I meant every word of it bitch. Tell her to get the fuck gone already."

"He can't talk to me like that, I live here too an-"

Smile.
Wave.
Shut the door.

Sorry.
Bitch.

Somehow I have a feeling that problems don't solve themselves this easily.

"So, let me get this straight. You truly believe that this Bob character has a chance of winning a national election and running an entire country? By all means, feel free to elaborate."

"Well, that's the thing. That right there. The fact you referred to Bob as a character rather than a candidate. This is what I think is especially important right now. An election has never faced a candidate like this. One who so fluently and consistently exists without the need to take any sort of stance. Historically, never before has such a situation been presented to the voters, and I believe it's worth acknowledging the significant role someone like this can play in an election. If not this one, most definitely in future ones."

"Possibly, but statistics have shown that never before has someone come out of nowhere - representing an entirely new political party - and had any chance whatsoever at even making any foothold within the political system as we know it. They've all faltered and ultimately failed. You seem to be suggesting that a rogue political party could gain enough momentum quick enough to survive, and - not only that - win on a federal level. That is frankly absurd, I'm sorry. If you look at the formation of any political party in the history of this country nowhere will you find an example to substantiate such claims, despite what sort of new fangled gimmick might be employed. A gimmick is not going to win the leadership of a first world country."

"Saying that this is a gimmick shows lack of respect where I think some should be due. I'm not saying Bob's going to win, but I am saying that Bob may set a dangerous precedent for the future - rogue or not - in how elections are run and how the public make

their decision on who to lead them. You're right, never before has anyone addressed politics in this manner with results, but I would argue that Bob is a different beast entirely."

"Elaborate."

"Gladly. Well, most noticeably he hasn't participated in any political debate, hasn't made any public appearances, hasn't agreed to be a part of any sort of televised or public events. More so, he hasn't made any sort of official political stance whatsoever, even in writing. Bob has shown no effort to prove that he even exists. Yet he does, and this can't be ignored because he has earned a circle on the ballot. This has never been done before."

"That may be so, but why would anyone possibly vote for a candidate who has no clear political stance, and furthermore - as you yourself just stated - may not even exist? It's ludicrous, really. I find it in no way logical that a percentage of the population - let alone a majority - would possibly draw their 'X' within a circle without knowing the man behind the name. I can't see how a sane person could possibly vote for a candidate who - for lack of a better term - may be a ghost. People don't vote for ghosts, Doctor, and I find it hard to believe that you would."

"I think what is more important is that statistically speaking, people don't vote in general, and if you can decipher the underlying reason why more than half the population didn't take part in electing our last democratic leader - whether he be ghost or man - then you can maybe devise a structure by which to win. There is a statistical lack of trust towards our fellow man, especially those within politics. I'm not defending a ghost - as you call him - just trying to point out that this ghost is filling a void which he may believe most of the population resides within."

"So, what you are saying is that Bob is trying to capitalize upon a majority that does not vote by purposely attempting to go against the grain of the electoral system? It's not as cut and dry as that, people aren't that predictable. There are many reasons why a person may choose not to vote."

"As are there many reasons a person may choose to take the time to draw an 'X'. All I'm saying is that even at this point I don't feel it would be logical to assume that - regardless of the outcome -

Bob won't make any sort of an effect upon the future of politics within this country. He approached this campaign from a perspective that arguably has never been attempted before and because of that we're sitting and having this debate right now, along with countless other people across the country. People asking themselves, 'Who is Bob?'. Many who have never even considered engaging in a political debate or discussion before now. I find it fascinating, regardless. I mean, can I ask you one thing? Can you at least admit that - one way or another - having a candidate like Bob has made this election far more interesting and widely discussed than any other that you can recall, ghost or not?"

"Well, I guess it's hard to deny that. So yes, but one could say that the addition of ghosts makes any story more interesting. Bob's presence has definitely had a significant impact on the political landscape within this countr-"

"Hey buddy, do you think you can change the radio station? I don't feel like listening to this political bullshit."

"I can, but I won't."

"Whatever. There goes your tip, I guess."

Fucking cab drivers. Fucking talk radio.
Fucking election. Fucking Spudley.
I need to smoke a joint.
I should really get smokes first.
Yeah. Need smokes.
Fucking Spudley, I wonder where he fucked off to.
Whatever.
Fuck him.
Smokes.
Where do they sell smokes along this stretch?
The Big Nickel.
Perfect.

"Can you pull in here for a second? I need to run in and get smokes."

"No problem."

"Got a light?"
"Yup, here. Spark it up."

Usually when I light a joint, I don't think about much else besides getting a nice clean cherry going - anticipating the smoke in my lungs, and the feeling it gives me - but my mind keeps veering towards Reef.

"You doing okay, Reef?"

Looking over from the doob and watching his head drop in thought a bit, it's safe to say he's not okay. No response required, but looks like he's going to say something.

That's good.

"Well, since you ask - no. No, I'm not."
"Yeah. I can tell. You want to talk about it? What's up? I mean, I'm not trying to pry but -"
"Fuck, I don't know, man. But - I'm not doing good."

Wait.
Wait for him to elaborate, he will. He needs someone to listen right now, not respond.

Give him time to compose his thoughts into words.

Fuck, dude. Look at this place.

You don't live like this unless something is seriously wrong, and you don't invite someone into a living space like this unless you want them to know that something is wrong.

A silent call for help.

There's no attempt to hide anything at this point - just a

struggle to reveal - and I've known Reef long enough to understand that.

Reef isn't happy, and that's definitely understandable.

Fuck. I get it.

It's funny how we can be stubborn about asking for help, instead trying to draw the offer out of friends through their environment. Giving people signs and desperate hints that they need help rather than say the words.

Reef was asking for help.

"Fuck, dude. I mean - it's like - fuck. Why are we playing this game? I'm trying to get it but I just don't fucking understand. Why the fuck are we here? I mean, it's - now that I'm old enough to kind of see the game for what it is, it's like - fuck, it's like - ummm.

"Okay, it's sort of like - ever play Monopoly? I mean, sure you have. Everyone has. Well, so you know how it works, and shit. Right? So - like - you know, you go around the board buying land, and charging other people rent when they land on your shit and blah blah blah.

"But yeah, so the only way to get your own land is by hitting an unowned space - not only that, hitting that spot with cash in pocket to fucking buy the thing - or by bartering with someone else and making a deal. But again, you need some cash or land up front. You need to use what you have in order to gain while taking whatever other people have yadda yadda yadda til one person owns everything and everyone else is fucking broke.

"For one thing, how the fuck can you call that winning? But for me it's this whole idea - this thing I can't fucking shake that - well, so the whole premise of this game - the thing that makes it fucking work as a game - is the fact that everyone starts on equal ground, right? The bank hands out your starting budget and it's a battle to claim the most and/or best property the quickest, right?

"Fun shit. Yeah well, fuck. Picture this: imagine jumping in late in the game, when half the property is owned. Your friends have been playing for a couple hours before you showed up, so they figure out how to include you, but this is a fucking game. As much fun as the game may be, the ultimate goal is to fucking win. How do you possibly stand a chance entering late? The game can't be made fair at that point. The best you can do is just teach the new players that the game itself isn't fucking fair by design. Fucking bullshit.

"So then, what about when the entire game board is already owned, and every bit of property is sitting safely within someone's possession? What the fuck is the point of joining as a new player when the game has mostly played out? Again, yeah maybe people will give you some money and land out of pity - to get you involved - but surely not enough to outweigh them or even come close. More than likely their generosity is merely a personal tactic that you're too new to the fucking game to possibly understand.

"Because, fuck. They still want to win. Even if they don't know why anymore. But we get thrown in fresh, during the end-game without any fucking resources available. Fresh fucking meat. What the fuck are you supposed to do? Your only option is trying to sprint your ass all the way around the fucking Monopoly board claiming that free 'Go' money - you know, the paycheque-to-paycheque life - or just giving the fuck up and landing in jail, where at least you can't be forced to pay fuckin' rent for a few turns.

"It's bullshit. I mean - the way I see it - this is the world we were born into. This. This fuckin' depressed generation that has nothing, and will only ever achieve the bare minimum to compete, despite obvious gifts and talents.

"Like, fuck. We know we've lost, yet we're still being forced to play. We're being fucking humoured, and we can't make them stop. I give up. I don't want to play anymore. Fuck this fucking shit.

"Can I quit without dying? I mean, I'm just - I'm tired of this shit."

He's done, but now he's waiting for me to say something. I - well - I ummm. I wasn't prepared for all this right now.

Say something, just speak,

"Well, of course you can quit without dying."

What? Really? That was a fucking empty effort at words.

Embarrassing, really.

"Yeah? How?"

An empty effort I just got called on.

Deer in the headlights.

Stiffened goat.

Fuck. I have no idea.

Just say it.

It's not what he wants to hear right now, but at least it's honest. Just say you have no idea.

Just fucking say it.

"Sorry, man. I have no idea."

"Remember the time when that idiot kid cut across the front yard, and I ran out and fuckin' punched him in the gut and exploded his stupid fuckin' kidney?"

Yeah, I remember. You fucking psychopath.

Laughing so hard right now at the memory you're fucking crying. That's not cool. You hurt that kid bad.

For no fucking reason.

I'm getting upset.

I should go. I should really go. Right now.

Cement saw smoke is still drawing a line in the air.

"Ruptured that stupid punk's kidney, right there."

Stop talking.

I hate picturing it. Stop making me.
I need to leave.
Now.
Right now.
Something bad is about to happen.
I need to go.

"Pow. That'll teach him to step on someone else's fuckin' grass. Hahaha. Inconsiderate fuck. You done rolling that fuckin' joint yet, you piece of shit?"

"I have to go."

"Go?"

"Yeah, I'm late for something."

Late for something? Really?
Well, that was lame.

"Late for being a bitch?"

Okay well, that was even more lame.
Fucking idiot. Whatever. I'm out.

"No, I just remembered I was supposed to meet someone."

Yup, someone. Anyone. Anywhere but here.

"Your boyfriend?"

Lame.

"Sure, whatever. Yes, my boyfriend. Here, you finish rolling it. There's a penis waiting for me."

"Ha! No problem, faggot. Have fun getting your asshole torn to shreds."

You too, Granger.
Your time is coming.

At least I really, really hope it is.
And I'd be best to establish my distance.
Such a fucking waste of flesh.

I feel like I'm running through mud trying to get the hell out of here fast enough.

Like in a dream.
My spidey sense is going off.
Colours that shouldn't be, flashing into my vision.

I need to leave.

It's like running to the bathroom when you have to puke.
I can't think anymore, I have to move.
Now.

Thoughts can wait.
Time for action. *GO*. Just fucking go.

Crashing out of the door into the fresh air and sunshine is only a brief victory.

I know I need to get entirely off of the property.
Farther away. Distance myself from the blast zone.
Farther.
Farther.

Keep walking.

Don't run.
Act calm.
Just keep going.

I'm probably overreacting anyway. There probably isn't any sort of imminent danger whatsoever.

It's probably all in my hea- oh?
Oh, wait.
What's that?

Two cruisers coming up the road.
Approaching.
I wonder if they're coming here.
To my place.
Of course they are.

I'm certain they are.

I left just in time.
They'll only find Granger.

I hope he tries to fight them.
I hope he aims for their kidneys.
Maybe then, things will finally change around here.

"Okay. So I guess it's safe to tell this story now. Since I'm not a part of it anymore."

Spudley takes a deep haul off the joint and blows his smoke across the beams of light stretching through my dimly lit place. I had completely forgotten about him, was too caught up in myself.
I feel like a jerk.
Put myself away for a moment.
Give notice to someone else.

"Fuck, sorry man. Yeah, what's up with you?"

"All good, no need to apologize. You've had a lot on your mind. I get it. But - so, yeah. Where do I begin? Well, basically the thing is - I've been doing these runs lately."

"Runs?"

"Yeah, through this Asian guy I met a few years back. Name's not important - whatever - but anyway, they give me this car, right? Trunk's been perfectly measured to fit a shipment. However many pounds of whatever - I really have no idea - but it slides in and fills the entire trunk."

He pauses - takes a puff - and just sits there staring into nothingness like he's expecting me to say something. I have nothing to say. I'm content just listening to the whole story first.

This is his moment.

So they give you a car to run shipments in.

Go on. I'm listening.

"So anyways, it's been a few months of this now. I drive out to the spot, get the trunk loaded up, and then go deliver it. Super easy. Only takes a couple hours in all, and I get five hundred bucks. Cash."

He crushes out the oversized butt of the joint in his mouth and sparks up another, larger one he'd been rolling from the shrapnel on the tray.

"So. last night."

Puff.

"I had picked up the package like normal and was heading out to drop it off, right?"

Puff, puff, pass.

"Routine shit. I've been to this particular place a few times, way out in the middle of nowhere. Has this long dirt driveway leading to this innocent looking rancher with just a couple trees around it and mostly farmland stretching into the shadows. Soybeans, I think. I don't know. Whatever it is, the crop doesn't grow very high, but that doesn't matter.

"So, anyway. Last night. I get to the house - and I'm turning into the driveway - and as the headlights pan across the field towards the house all of a sudden all I see is: *BAM.*"

He throws his hands up and begins miming across the air like he's laying bricks.

"Cop car, cop car, cop car, undercover, undercover, cop car. All across the front of the house. They had just fuckin' swarmed the place I guess, expecting the 'package' to already be there. The fucking package I was bringing. I fucking shat myself, dude. Fucking freaked right the fuck out."

He takes a shaky toke and finally passes the weed my way. I'm still intent on listening. Fill my lungs quick. Pass the talking stick back to him.

"Holy fuck. How are you not busted?"

Exhale. Listen.

"No fucking clue. Seriously. I panicked."

Puff, puff, panicpuff.

"I didn't even pull into the driveway. I just finished making a fucking U-turn. Turned right the fuck around and went back down the road where I came from, hoping that nobody would follow me. Just a random lost car in the night."

Puff, pass. He continued to speak while holding in air and smoke.

"Fuck, man. I kept looking back over my shoulders. I kept expecting at least one or two cars to chase after me."

Exhale.

"I kept picturing the headlights and cherries in the darkness behind me - flashing at me through the rear-views - and when I got farther away I started anticipating cops up ahead, like a roadblock or something. I just kept picturing cop cars rolling up from hidden side streets totally expecting me, floodlights in through the windshield on my face guilty as fuck. It was brutal, dude. So, I weaved through the boonies for a while and made my way back into town trying to avoid any main streets."

Story over? Grab the joint back from him, respond.

"Fuck, dude, that's crazy shit."

Puff.

"Yeah, man. So like, I didn't know what to do. I still had all the shit and everything in the trunk. I didn't want to call anybody either, right? I didn't know how big of a raid they were pulling or whose phones were tapped and shit. I was fucking paranoid as fuck, man. Still am."

Story isn't done. Return the stick. Resume listening.

"Oh, for sure. That's insane. 'Ere."

"Thanks. Yeah, man. So, finally I get a phone call on my cell - the one my boss gave me for this sort of shit - and the voice on the other end just says:

'Still got a load to drop?'

I'm like:

'Yeah.'

Then he gives me some random address and just hangs up. Sketchy shit, but I don't want to be responsible for this car and all this dope, right? So, I go to the fucking address and pick up these two guys."

Puff. Pass.

This joint just keeps burning. I can toke and listen.

Go on.

So you pick up these two dudes, then what?

I'm getting pretty baked.

"So these two dudes, right? Never seen 'em before. They just start directing me down streets and weaving me through neighbourhoods until they finally point out this big fancy house behind a fucking gate and tell me to pull in, right?"

Fancy house. Behind a gate. I'm listening. 'Ere. Take it.

He takes it. He tokes it.

"So, the gate just fuckin' opens. I pull up this driveway and the garage door opens right up, too. I end up driving this fucking thing right into the garage like I just completed an epic mission on Grand Theft Auto, man. I'm picturing the dollar signs rolling up in the top corner and shit. The package in the trunk the whole time. It was intense."

"Fuck, dude."

"Fuck indeed."

He pauses, and just sits there staring into space. Now is the story over? I thought he said he achieved the mission. Why would he have to lay low?

Inquire.

"Still doesn't explain why you need to lay low, though. Cops won't be looking for you, dude."

"Oh, right. No, that's not why I need to lay low. This is why I need to lay low..."

Spudley reaches into the crotch of his pants, pulls out at least a quarter pound of weed in a suffocated Ziploc baggie, and slaps it onto the table. I was wondering what was up with the baggy jeans on a hot day like this.

"I need to keep this safe. Somewhere it can't be found for a bit. Does your freezer work?"

"No power. So, think about it. You don't want to go near that thing. But - ummmm - what the fuck, dude?"

"Right. Well, want to smoke another one?"

"Of course, but -" he cracks the seal, releasing the pungent aroma of fresh weed into the air, "you still have quite a bit more 'splaining to do, Lucy."

"Cool, thanks. You can just let me out here."

"You sure?"

"Yeah, this is fine."

Cop cars at Bob's place. Not good.

"That's five-sixty."

Count out the exact change. Get rid of as much shrapnel as possible. Here you go fucker.

"Here. It's all there. Thanks. Cheers."

Fuckin' pigs.

Wonder what's going on. Best to just keep my distance. I'll just grab a seat on the curb, have a smoke and wait for them to leave. Engines are running, there's no sirens, and there's only two vehicles so probably just their stupid upstairs neighbour calling them over something trivial. Blah blah blah.

What a bitch.

That Granger guy is definitely a psycho, though.

Maybe they're finally taking him away. Nah, wishful thinking.

He's all balls and no brains.

And that's his problem. Not his crime.

I hope Bob's there. I hate being stuck alone there with Granger and his petty insults. It's just not a fun environment.

He's got good weed, though. So it keeps me coming back.

I know he shorts me on bags, too. Stingy prick, but not much I can do about it. I've seen worse. Some people spray their weed with Sprite or 7-Up to give it fake crystals. I've even heard of people adding a thin metal bar to Ziploc baggies to up the weight. All sorts of methods to trick the scale. At least Granger rips you off straight up.

He throws you a sack, you can take it or leave it. Most times you're stuck taking it, and he knows that.

But like I said, the weed is good.

Plus, options are scarce.

"So, go on. Continue the story. Where'd you get all that?"

"Well, I guess you could say that I pinched it. But, I would say that this was my fair cut for a long night's work."

"You fucking stole a quarter pound of weed? Great. You're a fucking dead man. You kn-"

"Listen. Wh-"

"Not smart, dude. I seriously thought you were smarter than that. Re-"

"Will you just let me f-"

"A quarter fucking pound?! That's way more than a pinch."

"Reef!"

"Yeah."

"Can I just finish telling my fucking story?"

"Sure, finish your fucking story. But at least pass that joint."

"Yeah, no problem but hide this. I'll roll another one too, out of this other stuff I've got. It's all good. Cool? So, anyway. We get to the other guy's house, right? Pull the car into the garage. Done deal. Mission complete, I thought. So, the three of us go in and the dudes there offer us drinks and shit, but we're not allowed to smoke any weed on the property. Anywhere in the fucking neighbourhood, for that matter. Crime-free Neighbourhood Watch thingy - whatever - but, we have a few drinks and then bring the package into the house and it gets to the point where I'm starting to tell the guys that maybe we should go and they start saying that we have to wait until morning to get another car. Bunch of bullshit. So I'm like, 'This is bullshit.' but what can I do? I'm stuck there.

"We keep having drinks, playing some pool and shit and the next thing I know, me and the other two dudes are trying to pass out in this unfinished room down in their basement where we've got the fuckin' package of weed stashed, right? Because the two dudes didn't completely trust the people whose house we're at, I guess. I don't know. I was pretty hammered and tired by that point. Fuck, I was just trying to make it through the night. It was cold, and I kept waking up now and then because I thought I heard someone at the door - I'm a really light sleeper, especially when I'm not comfortable - so, then eventually I noticed the door open, and one of the guys from the house creeps into the room. All sneaky and shit."

"What the fuck."

"Yeah, man. I just laid there and pretended to sleep. Even tried breathing slow and heavy like the other two dudes who I knew were out cold, but yeah, I saw him creep over - his fucking shadowy figure moving slowly across the room in the dark - and he cut into the fuckin' package. He sliced into that shit and then he just started pulling buds out, as quietly as he could. He filled his pockets, filled his hands, pushed the plastic back together a bit where he cut through, and then snuck out."

"Damn. That's pretty ballsy."

"Fuck yeah, right? Well, what's even more ballsy is that he came back fifteen minutes later with a plastic container thingy, and started shoveling buds right out of the package. I couldn't fucking believe it, and he had a pre-cut piece a tape that he stuck across the hole in the bag. Patted that shit into place and then left again. Shut the door and was gone."

"Ha damn, what a fucking slimy rat."

"Yeah well, that slimy rat got the wheels turning in my head. It was whatever-the-fuck hour in the morning, I was sleeping on the floor of an unfinished basement in some random house, and I still hadn't been paid for the bullshit I went through that night. I did my fucking job. As far as I was concerned, I delivered the package as best I could, right? So, I decided, 'Fuck this, I'm going to take my cut too and then I'm going the fuck home.' Fuck that shit."

"Aaaaaand so you stole a quarter pound of weed from organized criminals. Good story."

"Still not done, man. I have a plan. Just let me finish. Here, spark this one."

"Okay, go on."

"Okay, anyway. So. What I'm going to do is - I'm going to sell weed."

"You can't sell this weed, man. You'll definitely get caught."

"No, I'm going to ask him if I can start selling for him - start selling his shit - and get a front."

"A front?"

"Yeah, a front. Have him hook me up with a few ounces, show him how quick I can flip it. I know enough people who smoke dope, and I can drop my prices below anyone else while slowly mixing this bag in."

"That's crazy enough to work, actually."

"It's not crazy, it's smart. I'm out of a job, and I need a new one now. They trusted me with a car, so I'm sure they'll trust me with a bag of dope."

"But what if they suspect you stole the weed?"

"What kind of moron steals a bunch of weed in the middle of the night and then takes off suspiciously? Obviously it would make me the prime suspect."

"Yeah, but you did. And you are."

"But I'm not a moron. If I can prove that I'm not stupid enough to pull a stunt like that, I'm in the clear. The most obvious is the least obvious. Besides, if I stole the weed why would I turn around and ask for a job?"

"Because you're a clever piece of shit."

"Exactly. Not a moron."

"And we're not smoking a big huge blunt right now out of the weed you had me hide because -"

"Keeping up appearances, technically I don't have that weed to smoke. Gotta keep the doobs normal-sized for now. I suspect they could find me at any moment. Doubtful they'd find this place, but you never know."

"Yeah, and I hate you Spudley."

"Don't worry, Reef. It'll be worth it."

I keep sparking joints until my brain
acquiesces and retards.

"Bob here?"

"Who the fuck are you?"

I know this butt-fucker. I think this is that stupid Nutsack fuck. One of Bob's loser friends.

"Droopy Mc-Fuckin-Droopnuts. At your service."

"Yeah? Whatever, Nutsack. What the fuck do you want?"

"Is Bob here?"

Nope, fuck off.

"Nope, fuck off."

"Okay. Well, can I buy some green."

Money? I like money. Sure, Nutsack.

"Sure, Nutsack. I'll sell you some fuckin' dope. But you have to smoke one."

"Fine. What's that smell? Was there a fire?"

"Don't fucking worry about it. Come on in, fucknuts."

This stupid piece of shit is definitely getting a short bag. Fucking Bob rat faggot piece of shit fuck. I hope he comes home soon. I'm going to smoke this Nutsack dude's bag of dope and then beat the fucking piss out of that goof fucker right in front of him. Piece of shit. Fuck.

Try to get me fucking arrested. Fucking pig fucker. I know better than to let cops take me away for nothing. Rat fuck, sneaking away right before they show up. Fuck him. Fuckin'.

Fuck.

"Here you go, buddy. Thirty-five fuckin' bucks."

"For this?"

Excuse me?

Why this fuckin' little - he better just give me his fucking money or else I'll take the shit from him.

"Take it or leave it, man."

"No worries, I just can't roll a big one."

"Just give me the cash, fucker, and roll one up."

Fucking bitch. That's right. Give me your fucking money.

Piece of shit.

I really hope I'm pissing this fucking kid off, because I could really use an excuse to punch someone in the fucking face.

Try and get lippy, bitch.

KNOCK-KNOCK-KNOCK

What the fuck? Did this piece of shit fucking -

"Did you bring other people here you fucking faggot? Who the fuck's at my door?"

"No clue, man. Nothing to do with me."

"Yeah? Well go answer it, you piece of shit. Tell them I'm fucking busy."

Busy grabbing a knife to fuck up whoever the hell comes through that fucking door, that's what I'm busy with. Better not be Bob coming back here with his butt-loving cheese-dick faggot friends trying to defend his rat goof ass, I'll mess them all up.

Fuckin' fucks.

This sucks.
I should just go back home.
Has it been long enough yet? How long has it even been?
Definitely not long enough.
Fucking Granger.
Fucking cement saw.
I hate walking without having a destination.
I hate just killing time. Without a purpose.
Granted, I'm not the most productive person in the world.
I'm barely productive at all, really.
But still, time is important,
and right now mine's being wasted.
Is there anywhere I can go?
I could walk uptown,
but I just don't want to.
I don't feel like seeing people.
Talking to people.
Doing the whole 'people' thing.
I just want to go back home.

Where I was doing nothing.

Fuck.

I hate that place. It's home, though. I think I hate that, too.

I guess I mainly just hate Granger.

It would be different if he wasn't there.

I could maybe do things if he wasn't around.

Maybe.

Why the hell is he still there? And he's always there.

Always. Fucking. There.

Fuck. Seriously.

So sick of his shit. His stupidity. Him.

Hopefully the cops take him away.

That would be nice.

Yeah, right.

At best he'll get a notice to appear on a petty disturbing the peace or uttering threats charge. Can't really do much about him yelling at the neighbour, and it wouldn't be the first time. Unless he punches a cop. I hope he punches a cop.

Oh, please let him punch a cop.

If I could go home to an empty house, that would just make my day. Punch a cop, Granger. Punch a cop for Jesus.

Fuck.

Can I go home yet?

No. I should give it more time. Maybe I should go eat something. Grab a quick slice of pizza.

Make a mission out of this random vacation.

Force a destination.

I'm lazy, but I do like having a destination.

Fuck it.

Pizza it is.

I hope my timing's right.

Hopefully, my internal pizza clock is telling me they're putting in a fresh pie right now and I'll get to watch it as it's sliced up and slid into the warmer. Ready just in time for me to pick my favourite piece. I can see it now.

That one there.

No, not that one. That one.

Yeah.

Pizza is a good idea.

Then I can go home and listen to the fuckin' Granger swear about cops for a couple hours. On a full stomach.

Fun stuff.

Yeah, pizza. Definitely pizza.

I'll go out and get beer later.

Still early.

"Do you know who I am?"

"Ummm, I'm guessing you're the landlord?"

What other person could possibly be knocking on the door to this basement suite, with such confidence, and such a majestic, white beard?

It really is an impressive beard, I must say.

Bob wasn't lying.

"Are you guessing, boy? Well, I do run the land but unfortunately, I wouldn't be too quick to declare myself the Lord."

His hidden mouth movements make the whole beard shake.

Don't laugh.

"Okay then."

Don't laugh.

"And do you live here?"

Whatever you do, don't laugh.

Hahaha, but look at it! Look at it move!

No! Don't.

"No, sir."

"Yet you answer the door as if you do. Strange."

"Sorry, he asked me to. I'll go get him."

An escape. Good job soldier.

Get the Granger, this is his problem.

Abandon post.

The enemy shows far too much regalia.

Fuckin' weird, overly polite Santa Claus guy.

I don't know what to make of that landlord dude, and if his sentences had been any more polite and proper I wouldn't have been able to control myself.

Hahaha, that beard. So hard to take seriously.

Groomed like a perfect shrub.

Shrubbery. Too much. Oh, man.

How does he get it to look so perfect?

I should ask him.

No, fuck that, not talking to him anymore unless I have to.

Not my place, not my problem, Granger's issue to deal with. I'll just run down and grab him and th-

"Who the fuck is it?"

"It's your landlord, I think. He wants to talk to talk to you."

"The Santa Claus one or the Gandalf one?"

Hahahaha, oh shit. He said it, not me.

He totally looks like, well,

"Ummm, the, ummm..."

"Tell him to fuck off."

"You do it."

Doesn't he realize that this Saint Nick motherfucker can hear everything we're saying right now?

He must.

I don't want to be a part of this anymore.

Turn my gaze back to the beard at the top of the stairs, and the beard speaks.

"I would highly suggest he approach me personally. It's in his best interest to do so, and - for clarification - I would be the Santa Claus one."

'I would be the Santa Claus one.' oh shit, this is too much.

If there were milk in me, it would be coming out my nose right now. Arcing across the room in pearly fountains.

But seriously, this is just weird and completely not my fucking problem. Really. This old dude's just *'ho-ho-ho'*ing at me down the chimney with his old, creepy eyes.

Granger's sitting on the couch staring at nothing at all.

I'm the mediator between a moment that none of us want to exist within. Why?

Fuck this.

"Dude, go talk to your fucking landlord."

"Tell him to fuck off! Fuck!"

And now they're both staring at me. Well, staring at each other through me.

What the fuck am I supposed to even do right now?

This isn't in my job description. Like, fuck.

This isn't my fucking problem.

The whole reason I don't have a job is so I can avoid being responsible for things.

Things that really aren't my responsibility.

Such as this. Whatever is happening here.

Right now.

What is this shit? Why is it taking up my time?

What the fuck is going on here?

Where's Bob?

"I think it would be a better idea for him to come to the door, rather than telling me to 'fuck off', as he put it. I can hear him just fine and do not require a translator. Sorry, but if you are - in fact - my translator, I must say that you're not very good at your job."

This isn't my fucking job.

"Sorry, sir. I'll go get him."

"No need to apologize. I'll wait right here. You can tell him that, if you like."

I just need to get away from Santa's politely intimidating stare. Stop looking at me, I didn't do anything to end up on your naughty list. This is Granger's problem. I'm an innocent bystander.

So yeah, wait right there. While I translate...

"Dude!"

"What? Is he gone?"

"No, he still wants to talk to you. Just go fucking talk to him."

"Fucking pussy. Can't do fucking shit. All Nutsack, no fucking balls."

All nutsack? Fuck that. Go deal with your own shit. Not my fucking problem. You take the stairwell, you answer the door, you be the fucking translator, I'll chill on the fucking couch.

You're up Granger, show your balls.

That's right.

Get up.

Go.

Whip 'em out for Santa to see.

I'm watching.

"Hey, what the fuck are you still doing standing at my door?"

"Technically I purchased this door. So, it would be mine."

"Fuck you it is, I pay my fucking rent. Fuck off 'til the first, old man. Hear me?"

"There's no need for hostility. I just wanted to discuss the terms of tenancy with you regardi-"

"Write me a fucking letter and leave it in my mailbox. Get lost."

"I'd prefer to talk. I'm also a rather skilled neg-"

"I'd prefer to punch you in the fucking face."

"Really? With that hand there, and your frame? I would think you would want to prac-"

"Are you still talking? Get the fuck out here!"

"Hmmm. As you wish. I will remind you, though: this is my property."

"I pay rent, it's mine for now."

"Yours. For now. Yes. Well said."

"Whatever, old man."

"Indeed, young man."

Door slams.

Muttered swearing is heard beneath descending footsteps.

"Stupid piece of shit. Whatever, I fucking told him."

"I'm not so sure that you did."

"Yeah? Well, he won't be coming back here any time soon or I'll mess him up. Fuckin' old bastard."

"Yeah, I'm not so sure of that either."

"Shut the fuck up, Nutsack."

Gladly, I don't want anything to do with this fight.

I'm baked. That was some wicked weed Spudley's got.

Damn.

What time is it?

Holy shit.
He's been gone for a while now.
Been too baked to really clue in.
It was good talking to him, though.
Ha. What a fucking story.

Spudley gets all the stories...

What about me?
I should go do something.
Need to get out of this place more often.
Start living.

Live, Reef.
Stop acting like you're dying.
Go outside.

Where to go, though. Suggestions? Huh?

That's what I thought.

Easier said than done.

I guess I could go to the café for a while.
Grab a coffee, see who's hanging around.
That would kill some time.
Just need to kill the time. Time until I can go back to bed.

Fuck, Reef.
Stop sleeping, stop looking forward to sleep.
Stop dying.
Stop trying to kill time.
Stop thinking about death.

Death.
The darkness.
Pure.
Black.
Death.

Coffee.

Yeah, I need to get out.
I'm festering, and this isn't healthy.
It's not good for my mind.

It won't solve anything.

You know this.

Yeah, I know.

Stop dying, Reef.

I'm trying.

No, you're not.

Yeah, I know. I'll go out.
I'll get a coffee.

And what will that solve?

Stop it. Just - stop. I get it.
I do.

Fuck, I've really been letting myself fall apart.

I need to do something about this. I need to take better care of myself. Actually think about 'me' for once.

I haven't done that in a while.

No, you haven't.

Yeah, I know. Shut up.

Go somewhere.

Shut up. I'm going.

I should take some weed with me though. I mean, Spudley won't mind. Or know. Besides, that way if I get uncomfortable I can go smoke one somewhere instead of crawling back home. It'll help me stay out longer.

I need a change of environment.

A bit of time away from myself and my thoughts.

Good idea.

Yeah, I know.

Spudley knows how to get in if he comes back before me, anyway.

I'm sure he's out on another adventure.

Another story.

It's time for me to find my own.

"Spudley! There you are. We've been looking for you, bro. You been ducking us? Not cool."

Eyes stare outwards at me from a nondescript black car.

They're here. Okay. Here we go. Let's do this.

I wonder if they'll let me smoke in the car.

Doubtful.

Don't panic. Stay cool.

This is exactly what was supposed to happen. I've got this. Just need to stay cool. I know what happens next. I know what I need to do. The plan is sound. Stick with the plan. Don't panic. Follow to the script. Read the lines, as rehearsed,

"Ducking you? Why? I've got no reason for that, man. What's up?"

I know what's up. I know exactly what's up. You guys were the ones who entered the scene late. I've been walking around town for nearly an hour now and you guys were suppos-

"Boss wants to talk to you."

He looks to see if anyone is in earshot.

There isn't.

He continues.

"Apparently, there was an issue with the shipment."

That's an understatement. I know this. My character knows this. Stick to the script. Keep reading the lines.

Stay in character.

"Fuckin' rights there was an issue with the shipment. Like, a hundred cops were sitting at the house waiting for the drop."

Play dumb. Play dumb in front of the dummies. Shine under the cameras.

That whole night spent planning, questioning, analyzing the possibilities and outcomes. The plan is sound. Don't panic. Just stay in character. Stay within the scene.

Stick with the plan. Stick to the script.

They assume I'm a thief but their assumptions carry no weight. I know this. My character must remain aloof for now. They're just here to escort me, their opinions don't matter. Stick with the plan, the plan is sound.

Follow the script.

"Nah, not that. Something else. Boss says he's missing product."

Yes. Of course he is. Boss suspects me. Boss has to suspect me. This is normal, this is part of the scene. They're just reading their lines. I have to keep reading mine. Playing my role.

Don't break character.

"Missing product?"

I say with confusion. A blank stare painted across my face.

Don't panic.

Stay cool.

Stick to the script.

"Yeah, and that you went missing, too. Get in."

Muscles flex. Glances exchanged.
Don't break character.
Stick to the script.

"Ah, I see. Fair enough. Probably just a misunderstanding."

Hold eye contact.
Remain stoic.
Don't panic.

The boss is where the test comes into play. This scene is easy. This is just my ride. These people aren't here to judge my character. They don't even know how.

Act One. Spudley Gets A ride.

Act Two is where the play really begins. As long as everyone sticks to the script. Follows their lines.

It's your line, buddy. Keep the scene moving.

"Misunderstanding. Yeah. Just get in."

Close the line with a firm glance. Authoritative. Final.

"No worries. I'm getting in."
"Put that smoke out."

Damn.

"No worries."

I open the car door.
I get in.
I close the car door.
We drive off in silence.
The scene ends.

The curtains draw.

Won't be so easy with the boss. He won't be sticking to the script. He's going to be testing me on all fronts. I've had enough time to analyze a variety of possible questions and answers - problems and outcomes - but there's no way to fully predict another individual.

Especially one who isn't fooled easily.

He's the boss for a reason.

Don't underestimate him.

Don't panic.

Stick to the script.

Don't break character.

Wish I could've finished that smoke.

Granger's definitely a weird guy.

No, weird is too polite. Fucked up is more honest.

Don't know what to make of him, really.

I mean, right now the guy's marching around the basement suite with no particular intent.

He's just walking around, looking at things.

Like a soldier on guard, impressed by the kingdom that surrounds him. Surveying the beer can battalion. Making sure the ashtrays don't get out of line. All his smoke butt soldiers.

Bent and broken.

Into the bedroom, out of the bedroom, across the living room - checking to see if the poster looked at him funny - into the kitchen - swearing at the silverware sitting stagnant in the sink - back into the living room. Marching.

Making his rounds.

"Four o'clock, and all's well."

Back into the kitchen.

The fridge opens.

Some mumbles, amidst swear words.

Back into the living room, triumphant. Cracks a bottle of beer and starts to chug the entire thing back.

Wait.

Wait a fucking second...

Where'd he get the -

I recognize the bottle.

No.

It can't be.

This is not good.

All is not well.

All is definitely not fucking well right now.

No. Oh fuck, no.

Sound the alarms. Abandon ship. Abandon fucking ship!

He's finishing it.

Oh, fuck. He's finishing the beer from the fridge.

There it goes.

The last of the liquid drains out of the bottle like an hourglass. Granger's enormous Adam's apple rises to accept the offering, takes hold of the fluid, and then drops from the tree.

Eyelids crash together.

Time crawls.

I see every little moment happen in more detail than I want to. Oh, fuck. He drank it all. He fucking drank it all.

Why am I still being punished for this somehow?

Fuck you, Bob.

Seriously, fuck you.
This was supposed to be you, not Granger.
No-no-no-no-no-no-noooooooo. Fuck.
His eyes open.
He's looking at the bottle.
I can see him thinking about what he just drank.
Questioning it. Tongue analyzing the walls of its cave. Eyes squinting. Looking at nothing. Thinking.
This isn't good. This isn't fucking good.
He wasn't supposed to drink it.
I couldn't stop him.

Fuuuuuuuuuuuuuuuuuuuuuuuuuuck.

I know that look. I know it because I made it myself.
When I drank that bottle at the bulrushes.
When I slapped my tongue around my own mouth searching for clues, questioning what I just drank.
I know exactly what he's thinking right now.
He knows, but he doesn't.
He has a feeling, but he doesn't want to believe.
It couldn't possibly be true.
Could it?

"What's with this beer?"

You know.
Deep down you know exactly what's wrong with that beer.
You weren't supposed to be the one to drink it.
It wasn't yours.
What do I say? Do I say anything?
Time is passing, the clock is ticking, what do I do?
The Jeopardy music plays through a dying organ.
Time's running out.
Ah, fuck it. I'm a pussy, and this isn't my fight.
Sorry, Bob.
He doesn't know what happened out at the bulrushes that

day. He doesn't know what you did.

You played dumb when I asked.

I can play dumb too,

"What do you mean?"

He's thinking.

Analyzing.

Coming to conclusions but denying them.

Staring at the beer.

Staring at me.

Staring at the beer again.

"Nah. This doesn't taste right. It was flat or something."

"Well, that sucks."

Thinking about it.

Putting the pieces together.

But it can't be.

There must be another answer.

"It didn't make that 'psssshhhh' sound when I opened it. It didn't make any sound."

He knows, but he doesn't. There is no other answer.

Now I know how Bob felt.

This wasn't supposed to happen.

This is still all his fault.

He's waiting for me to say something. Say something.

"Maybe the seal was fucked up?"

"Nah, man. Something was up with this beer. Seriously. That didn't taste right,"

He's putting it together.

"it almost tastes like,"

He's almost there.

"like it was,"

Here it comes.

"like it was piss or something."

There it is. There's the secret word. Play dumb. I don't know why it would be piss. Why would I know?

"Piss? Why would it be piss?"

I know why it's piss.
I know exactly why.
Fucking Bob.
This is all his fault.

This fucking pizza tastes like ass.
Damn it.
It's always hit or miss, but I usually have better luck than this. Like, what the fuck? This is disappointing.
Nah, fuck disappointing. This is bullshit.
I should just fucking complain.
Carry these wedges of flavourless cardboard back in there and slam them down, demanding to see a manager.
No.
Nevermind.
It's not worth it. I've already left anyway.
It's not that bad, really. Just a bit old.

It's fine.

Fuck that, this pizza is shit. Probably be sitting around since they opened up this morning.

The last slices from the first 'za of the day, getting wrinkly under the heat lamp while waiting for me to show up.

And save them.

At two bucks a pop.

Fucking bullshit.

Cheese is cold.

Sauce is chalky paste underneath.

Look at that shit. My bite marks shouldn't carve so perfectly through a slice of pizza - that one tooth is getting more crooked - and it shouldn't take so long to chew afterward.

Damnit. This sucks.

The birds can fucking have this shit.

I'm not going to continue torturing my taste buds like this.

They deserve better.

What a waste of money.

Money and time.

Fuck.

Seriously.

I feel like someone, somewhere owes me something right now. Time, money, or pizza.

Fuck this. I'm going home.

I've wasted enough things already for one day.

I just had this thought...

I've never been full of myself.

Full of *me*.

Whenever I feel myself start to fill up inside I tend to trade it off to people at a discount price, or blindly sell some of me to the lowest bidder. It's just something that's never been much of a concern to me.

I mean, how do you really put a price on a piece of yourself? A piece that is created naturally just by being you. What value does that really have? It just doesn't make sense to me.

Seems wrong, like any price is too much.

I guess it's like a clam giving away its pearls. It wouldn't know how to calculate a value on something it just naturally creates. To the clam the pearl is just a piece of waste created from being. How could it be perceived as valuable? I used to think this was a good - even admirable - quality. Taking scoopfuls of myself and handing it out like penny candies. All with a smile.

Giving. Sharing. Helping.

Trying to be a good person.

That's what I'm doing, right? Right?

I mean, nobody wants to be full of themselves, right?

There's so many people who seem so empty. I had never known what it felt like to actually be empty. It was a foreign feeling to me to be scraping the bottom of the barrel trying to find some forgotten fragments that haven't been shelled out.

There's always been something there. Some more of me, within a seemingly bottomless container.

Not anymore.

I can feel the emptiness.

The warning signs were there,

but the language was unfamiliar.

Letting hands reach freely into the jar.

Trusting. Turning my back.

Blind generosity.

Sometimes people take too much. Pull too freely and quickly from the source not giving it time to replenish.

It's a hard thing to learn until it happens. It's easy to give until you give too much. When you're empty and waiting for pieces of yourself to start refilling inside naturally you can't help but think about all the pieces that were given away. Wasted.

In blind generosity.

Fuck.

I can't help but think about it.

I could use some of that 'me' back again right about now. I wish I could demand it back - go back and request the proper payment and cash in on the me that is owed back to me - but it doesn't work that way. Those pieces are gone.

Consumed. Assimilated. Broken down and reconstituted.

Turned into their pieces.

I don't want their pieces, I want my own.

The only way is to make new pieces but I haven't been able to. It seems like they refill faster when there's already something in the tank. It will grow exponentially. I just need to create the initial spark of life.

I need to turn the machines back on.

Dust off the recipe.

Get to work.

I need to do something, but I have no idea what that something is.

I've forgotten how to make it. The procedure.

How to make more of me.

Or,
maybe I just don't want to make it anymore.
Or,
maybe I'm simply lacking the source material.
Or,
maybe the recipe has changed somehow.

Whatever the reason, this emptiness is making me pine to be full again.

Full of myself.

Full of me.

When I think about it from this perspective I wonder what's so wrong about being full - full of myself - and what could possibly be admirable about willingly draining that resource.

There's no honour in acquiescence.

I'm an idiot.

An empty idiot.

Who forgot how to make myself.

An empty vessel.

...the door is a jar.

I'm not even a decorative jar worth putting on the shelf.

I'm a jar with a use, though.

I'm not broken.

I still have capacity.

I just need to remember what I am.

What my ingredients are. What I'm made of.

Jump start the system. Remember myself.

Focus.

Refill.

And then only give out pieces of me that overflow from the top. The surplus.

First thing though,

is to climb up out of this rut,

Reef.

Stop thinking about ghosts and start thinking about yourself.

I know. I'm trying.

Well, I'm starting to try.

I know this now.

The café is void of life, but still busy with people. Their mindless chatter invading my peace. Faces attached to characters that I care nothing about. Spewing distant words that I can feel penetrating my mind with unheard banality.

I need to go someplace else.

Where I can think more clearly.

Positively.

The bulrushes.

Yes.

That would be a good place to go chill - with a six-pack and my thoughts - and sort some shit out.

"Can I get you a refill?"
"No, thanks. I'm good."

Check, please.

It was piss. I drank fucking piss.

"I just drank fucking piss!"

I'm going to kill that fucker.

"I'm going to kill that fucker when
he gets back. That's fucking sick."

What the fuck?

"What the fuck? Why the fuck
was there even a bottle of piss
in the fridge to begin with?"

That's fucked up shit.

"That's fucked up shit, man.
Fucked up shit. Fuuuuuuuck."

I'm going to kill him.

"I'm going to fucking kill him.
I'm going to fucking kill him.
Stop fucking laughing."
"Sorry, man. I can't help it."
"Yeah well I won't be able to help
kicking the shit out of your Droopy
ass either. Fuck both you guys."
"Hey, man. I didn't do anything."
"Fuck that shit. Why the fuck
was there a beer bottle full of
fucking piss in my fucking fridge!"
"Calm down, man. Shit, you drank
that whole thing too, didn't you?"
"Shut the fuck up!"
"How did you not notice?"
"Shut up! Stop fucking laughing!"
"Sorry. Let's just smoke a joint or
something. I'll roll one up, just ch-"
"Fuck that. I'm waiting for this fucker
to get home. Fucking make me drink piss.
Fuck that shit. Piece of fucking shit.
I'm going to stand right fucking here
and just wait for him."
"You can't just stand there waiting
at the door for him to walk through it."
"Watch me."
"Yeah? How long can you really stay fully
tensed up like that, locked in kill mode?"
"You don't want to fucking know. I'm going to be
the first thing this little piss jester sees
when he walks through that fucking door."
"Your veins are popping and shit."
"Good."
"And the broken broomstick?"

"I'm going to either make him drink piss,
or beat the shit out of him."

I can wait all day, fucker.
But I know I won't have to.
You're a predictable piece of shit, if anything.
You'll be back here any fucking second now.
Predictable fucking piece of shit.

"He's a predictable piece of shit. He'll be back soon."

Mission: Accomplished.

Man, I love weed.
It's just a beautiful plant.
And the smell. Damn.
This weed smells so fucking good.

It's actually cutting through the stale air in this place and adding a bit of freshness.

Fuck, just look at this weed. This is some nice fucking weed.

I definitely won at life today. All this is mine. I wish Reef were here. Wonder where he went. I wanted to tell him my story.
How it all went down.

I guess that will have to wait.
Just look at this beautiful fucking weed.
The hairs. The crystals.
Buds hold so much character and variety to them,
like varieties of opals.
I could stare at a nice nugget for hours.
It's like porn almost.
Mmmmmm, weed porn.

Can't wait to look at this stuff under better light. This will have to do. At the moment, this is still the safest place. Running into Reef this morning was an unexpected bonus.

Another fortunate circumstance.

Yeah.

Today worked out surprisingly well, I must say.

That smell, though. The fragrant aroma that fills the air when you break open the seal. This shit is pungent. Fuck, yes. I've always wondered how anyone could find the smell of weed offensive. I mean, just smell that. Makes my mouth water.

Who wouldn't like that smell?

Okay well, I guess I kind of find the smell of flowers offensive. Certain smells just aren't for everybody, but I could easily see weed being used artificially for candles and essential oils. Companies using different strains, recreating a wide variety of fresh bud aromas through incense. It's a calming smell to have hanging in the air. At least in my opinion.

"Purple sticky punch."

I don't know.

I should smoke one while I'm doing this. It's hard to handle this much weed at once and not want to roll one up. I know it's best to weigh it all out first and separate it but, come on. I've waited long enough, I think. It's about time I enjoy the fruits of my labour.

I've earned this.

Yup, fuck it. I'm rolling one. I have to.

Damn.

This weed is extremely nice. Dense. Cured perfectly. A bit crunchy, but not too much so. Look at those hairs.

I don't know, I guess you could argue that it's a little too dry - if I had to find an argument - but it's perfect for weight. It'll make the bags look bigger. Still fluffy, kinda. Whatever, it's not hard to add a bit of moisture with a piece of lettuce or celery.

I wouldn't, though.

No need to with this weed. It would be disrespectful.

Why mess with it? Don't fix what isn't broken.

Love it for what it is.

Don't ever change, girl. You just do you.

spark

Yes.

This.

Ah.

So much fun handling this much weed, too.

Fuck, look at it all.

Look at you, girl. All of you.

I could just swim in you. But, no.

Time to get to work.

I shouldn't even be smoking any until it's all split up proper.

The first step is to take inventory.

I can't wait.

I can't wait until everything's bagged up.

I can't wait to see what I have. Quantified.

Everything beyond the last ounce proper is mine to smoke tonight. My reward. Hopefully Reef makes it back.

He's going to want to take part in this session.

It's always better to celebrate with friends, and Reef could definitely use some positive energy right now.

Oh, shit. Right. Reef. His Dad. All of that stuff.

That explains this place. That explains a lot actually.

Sorry, Reef. I was too caught up in my own shit.

Wasn't even thinking about your problems.

What you're going through.

Poor guy. I couldn't even imagine.

With his Dad dying, and all.

That's pretty heavy stuff.

I need to eat.

Starving.

Yeah. Food.

I'll pack this up for now and go grab some Chinese food. I'll get a bunch of shit. I'm sure Reef would appreciate it. Tonight, we celebrate and forget our troubles.

I guess I'll just stash this bounty, and deal with it later.

Never piss in someone's beer.

That's what the broken broomstick being held aggressively in my face was trying to tell me, but I didn't know that yet.

Granger was standing at the bottom of the stairs - foaming at the mouth - with the stick held firmly. Waving it around at me like a magic wand. A wand that could cast spells of pain, no doubt.

Piss and beer.

I didn't connect the two things as he yelled obscenities at me. Spraying spit and swinging around his splintered dowel.

Nope.

The difference between alcohol and urine wasn't really a factor at that particular moment. That sort of information didn't register on my radar at all.

"You're fucking disgusting! Fucking sick. Fuck you! Fuckin' sick piece of shit. Fuckin' fuck!"

Confusion.

Woah, okay. What the fuck did I do?

"Wait a minute, what the fuck did I do?"

I can hear full bore laughter coming from deeper in the suite. The struggles for breath between long bouts. It sounds like Droops but I don't see the connection. I still can't figure out what the fuck is going on. I'm missing something here.

I don't feel like I'm being given enough clues.

"Fucking sick! That's fucking sick! Fuck this bullshit! Stop fucking laughing, Nutsack!"

"What? What the hell happened?"

"It was piss! It was fucking piss! Fucki-"

"What was piss?"

"-piss! Your last fucking beer! Fucking sick! You're fucking sick!"

Broomstick flailing, laughter sputtering away, Pantera whining through the boombox. Wait a second, he drank my last -

"Wait a second. You drank my last bee-"

"It was piss! Fucking piss! I drank piss because of you! You're fucking sick!"

His voice always rose to sharp heights when he was angry, or excited for that matter, or pretty much any time his energy level was running high. He was completely furious at the moment like a foaming, rabid dog shrieking away. It always reminds me of that evil toon from Who Framed Roger Rabbit...

"Did he talk JUST! ...LIKE! ...THIS?!"

Yes. Yes, he did. But, wait a second. This doesn't make sense sense. He's mad at me because he -

"Wait, but you drank my last b-"

"It was piss! *Fucking piss*!"

"Yeah. Piss. I get that. But -"

"I drank piss! *Because of you*! Fucking sick!"

Piss? What he's saying is starting to sink in...

But that could only mean -

of course.

Oh fuck, eh?

So he -

Well, then. He did have a point there, I guess.

Barely.

Really, it's his own damn fault for drinking my beer.

It was piss, though.

Hahaha. Smooth move, Droops.

It's definitely because of me. Granger drank piss because of me. It's my fault that my last beer was replaced with a sealed bottle of urine. Damn.

A sealed bottle of urine.

Clever.

Almost got me. Actually, it would have got me eventually.

Although, maybe this fate is worse than if I would've just cracked that beer myself like was intended.

Granger staring me down with the intent to kill. This wasn't intended. None of this was intended. Right from the beginning.

Shit, how long has it been now since that day at the bulrushes? Three or four months at least.

Yeah. Shit, eh?

Hahaha. I've been on guard for quite a while now.

But Droops, hahaha. Good show.

Now Granger drank piss.

I shouldn't laugh. It was a stupid idea, and it's Droops getting the last laugh now. The show's still going for him.

That fucking day at the bulrushes is forever burned in my mind.

I don't know why the fuck we thought it would be funny to piss in Droops' beer when he left to go get munchies. Or, why I ended up being the one to do it. I've looped the memory too many times. Nothing new to learn. Nothing that could have been done differently. What happened happened.

I guess I was the only one who had to pee at the time.

For some stupid reason, we had this idea that when he got back and went to drink the piss beer we would stop him at the last moment and go, 'Ha! Don't drink that! It's pee!'

Smack it out of his hand and have a good laugh about it all.

We honestly thought that was how it would play out. We visualized it as a group and thought that it was a funny idea.

Real fucking funny.

Fuck, how drunk were we? Not very bright.

But, hindsight and all.

Twenty-somethings, right?

So - naturally - by the time Droops got back we had completely forgotten about the piss beer. No memory whatsoever. We were deep in conversation about some sort of trivial nonsense when he came back and went to take a swig.

Nobody was paying attention.

Until he said the words...

"What's with this beer?"

Silence. Guilty fucking silence. I got that feeling inside like being on an elevator that's started to move.

Plunge.

Down.

This was not good.

This was seriously not good at all.

"Seriously, guys. Did someone fuck with my beer?"

He examined the taste inside his mouth and poured out the rest of the bottle. It flowed clear from the neck into the dirt.

Slow motion lip smacks that keep playing in my mind.

"There was definitely something wrong with that beer. Seriously guys."

No one would say it. We all just stared at him, silent.

It would take days for someone to finally spill the beans.

Fucking, Spudley. But no, it's not his fault.

It was piss. It was fucking piss...

"*IT WAS FUCKING PISS*! Fuck this! This ends right fucking now! This is bullshit! *This shit ends right fucking now!*"

That shrill voice again.

Snap back to reality.

Focus gathers upon the weapon brandished.

Reality.

Granger.

Broomstick.

Happening.

Now.

Immediate response required.

Granger throws the broomstick to the ground. I have nothing. Deer in the headlights. Defenseless.

Bring on the pain.

I'm ready for him to rush me but he turns away and storms into the kitchen, mumbling under his breath.

What's happening?

I could just turn and leave right now, but I'm curious.

Leave.

No. I'm curious. What's he doing?

Follow him into the kitchen. Granger's slamming his way through all the cupboards, looking for something.

What's he looking for?

What's going on?

He grabs a dirty mug from beside the sink, waking up a cloud of fruit flies. The mug cuts through the mass as he turns back towards me.

What's going on?

"You're fucking drinking piss! This is bullshit! You're fucking drinking piss right fucking now!"

"Wait, what the -"

"Yeah! I'm going to go fill this fucking mug with piss! My fucking piss! And then I'm going to watch you drink the whole fucking thing! This is fucking bullshit! You're drinking fucking piss!"

No. No, I'm not.

Fight or flight.

The bulrushes

I didn't realize how much I needed this right now.

So many memories made out here.

So much energy put into this place.

We used to come here as kids. I lived nearby, on Pearl Street. It was just a five minute jog from my house - following the older kids on bikes - through our neighbourhood toward a dead-end which opened up into a cornfield. The corn wasn't there when I walked past, maybe there isn't any this year.

Such a chill path.

It splits the field from the yards. We would follow it to where it met up with the old train tracks.

Almost where I am now.

Still looks pretty much the same.

The tracks had been removed before I ever knew about this place, and their path was marked with cinder block checkpoints to prevent anything of decent size passing through. Dirt bikes never had trouble, and though I rarely saw them. Their paths ran everywhere like deer trails through snake grass.

None this year, though.

I remember, the rows of corn thinned out and the land turned to marsh by the time you reached the tracks. The other kids would find a patch of bush to stash their bikes, and we'd continue onward.

To your left it quickly became a swamp pebbled with islands of grass and cattails. Gnarly trees would spider up over the reeds.

One of these was an old weeping willow.

We would forge paths through the thicket towards it.

It was a landmark that you could see over the reeds no matter your age, and it drew us like a lighthouse. I remember us all trust-falling into the growth and allowing our weight to crush down the brush, so that we could trek a few more feet forward.

It was a lot of work, and every year the paths needed to be blazed again through the new growth.

I wonder who the neighbourhood kids are now, who maintain the path, and I wonder if they are as ignorant as we were to the service it provided other people after. The older people. After they had run back home for evening dinner served ceremoniously around the family table. Like me.

The dark side of the bulrushes.

I never come out here during the day anymore. The children work that crew. Whoever they are.

We punch in at night, and build paths outwards from the beacon tree. Making hangout spots that branched outward from their childish paths. Flattening out large areas - with pieces of wood like were were designing crop circles - and opening up enough space to have a fire surrounded by lawn chairs.

The chairs were taken from one of the yards that backed onto the footpath. A matching set of six positioned in an arc, with a large fallen willow branch completing the circuit. You could easily seat ten people here. I'm pretty sure there were ten of us here the night Bob pissed in Droops' beer.

Fuck, I still can't believe he did that.

Funny shit, though.

I don't think we've come out here as a group very often since then, actually. Granted it was winter and all, but that usually doesn't stop us from making a few trips out here. Regardless.

This place has a pull to it.

A feeling.

I missed this.

It's definitely been a while.

Fuck, I really needed this. I guess I didn't realize just how cooped up and depressed I've been.

The walk was energizing. The fresh air's invigorating.

This is...nice.

I think I'm actually beginning to feel like myself again.

Damn, Reef. I missed you.

Well...I missed me, too.

If you/me know what I mean, which obviously you both do.

I guess, people - it seems - don't have this sort of relationship with themselves. This sort of communication.

Ha.

I have a friend inside who is me - the other me, the retrospective hindsight version of myself - who always keeps his wits about himself and is never swayed by emotion or sporadic curiosities.

Those things are necessary, but aren't part of my deeper more logical self. Everyone's internal best friend is different. I'm only articulating from experience, but it's weird to think about the possibility of that person inside being an enemy.

You're not my enemy, are you?

Of course not.

Of course not.

Fuck. I had forgotten about him - me? - entirely and how important he is to my well-being.

All we do is argue, I've stopped listening.

Been completely ignoring myself.

Sorry, me.

No worries.

The mind sure is a confusing garden to wander through, but I'm addicted to its beauty. It's nice to be reminded of the beauty outside, though. External stimulation.

Fuck.

And even out here, I can't seem to get away from these "VOTE

BOB" signs. Who carried one all the way out here just to chuck it in a bush like this? Odd.

There's another one.

These things are truly everywhere.

I should bring this one with me,

as kindling for later.

Good idea.

Thanks.

No way I'm drinking piss.

While he's in the bathroom filling the glass I'm getting the fuck out of here. Fuck this. I'm out.

Droops is in my way. Skinny Puppy is now blaring in the background.

This isn't going to end well.

Get out of my way, Droops. I need to go. While I can.

"Now is the only thing that's real."

"I don't think so, man. This ends now."

Shit, seriously?

Fucking Droops. He's standing there blocking my path to the stairs with a stupid grin on his face. He's been waiting for this moment. There's no way he's going to let me leave.

This ends now. I get it.

Fucker.

The bathroom door flies open and Granger steps out with a full mug. I'm reminded of the image from Fear And Loathing.

Of Dr. Gonzo kicking open the bathroom door.

Drugged up with a knife in hand.
This is pretty much the same thing.

"What the fuck's going on here?"
"He was trying to leave."
"I don't fucking think so, you piece of shit. You're drinking piss."

No I'm not.

"Yeah, dude. You are."

Shut up, Droops. Fuck.
What the fuck do I do now? There has to be a way I can talk myself out of this, or at least talk it down a bit.
Fuck.
A mug of Granger piss is bullshit.
Just the sight of it makes me want to puke.

"...keep your eyes open, soft-spoken changes nothing."

"Guys, seriously. This isn't even fair. You want me to just knowingly drink a full glass of Granger's piss?"
"Fucking right, bitch! And no fucking chaser either. No pussy shit. Chug the whole thing."
"Granger, that's a bit extreme, don't you think?"
"Fuck that shit. *I fucking drank piss! I fucking drank that whole damn bottle!*"
"Yeah, but he has to knowingly drink piss. He has to put warm piss to his mouth and willingly drink it. And we get to watch and enjoy. Besides, the piss you drank was chilled. I say just a shot of piss should be good enough."
"Whose fucking side are you on, Nutsack?"
"I'm just saying th-"
"Nah, fuck that. *The whole fucking mug!*"
"That's a lot of piss, dude."

Fuck, at least Droops is showing a bit of reason.

"Yeah. I suppose I can agree to a shot of piss."
"*No. Fuck that!* You're drinking this whole fucking thing!"
"Granger, seriously."
"*Fuck that! The whole fucking glass!*"
"Dude!"
"I'll just get a shot glass, fuck."
"*The whole thing! You're drinking my fucking piss, bitch!*"

This went on for about as long as you would expect.

"Now is the only thing that's real."

"Reef?"

No answer.

Hmmm, he's still not back. But I'm getting the hang of climbing in and out of this window.

Carrying Chinese take-out food and everything.

Multi-tasking. The theme of the day.

Birds and stones, and all that jazz.

This has definitely turned out to be a good day. When I woke up yesterday I was relying on the food in my parents' fridge and looking forward to the delivery job lined up for after they went to bed. Now, here I am with like a half-pound of weed, five hundred bucks, a new job, and a very reasonable time frame in which to flip some product.

Yup, this calls for a celebration.

I deserve this.

But fuck, wish Reef were back. There's no way I can eat all this by myself. Wonder where he is. Probably a good thing, though. That he's out and about.

Dude needs some fresh air.

And I'm fine with a quiet night alone picking at all this food.

I don't even remember what I ordered.

A bunch of stuff.

A bunch of stuff, with extra deep fried prawns, and some Szechuan chicken.

Fucking love Szechuan.

Reef is seriously missing out.

Oh well, I guess it looks like it's going to be a quiet night by candlelight. Just me and Mary Jane, and enough takeout food to feed an average family.

And Mary doesn't eat much.

She just stimulates my appetite.

Sorry, babe. We can't watch a movie or anything.

Power's out. Storm or something.

We'll just have to enjoy each other's company.

I'll light a few candles and tidy up the table a little bit - set the mood, so to speak - and then I'll lay out the dinner.

I wonder if they put some plastic forks in here.

Was never one to fuck around with chopsticks.

And I wonder what my fortune is.

Let's see...

They gave me five cookies.

Fuck yeah.

I will choose my fortune like a god tonight.

Fucking Granger.

Fuck him, and his fucking piss.

And Droops, too.
Just standing there watching with that smug fucking face.
I need beer, and fast.
Ugggghhhh.
Why's the beer store so far? And why are my damn legs so slow. Need to get the memory of this taste out of my mouth.
So fucking gross. Fuck.
At least I managed to get Granger to agree to the shot rather than the whole damn mug.
A mug of piss. Fuck that.
And he even let me mix in a bit of Jack Daniel's.
Thank fuck I had that bottle lying around.
For a rainy day.
Golden showers.
Gross.
All in all it wasn't that bad.
Yeah it was.
Fuck those guys.
And fuck this 'Bob' guy, too. Using my name on his fucking signs all over the place.
Dick.

'VOTE BOB'

Yeah? Fuck you. Stop telling me what to do.
Not in the mood right now.
Stupid things are everywhere.
At first, I liked 'em. I mean, all dark and evil looking and telling people to vote for me? Fuck yeah!
I can get on board with that.
I'm smelling what you're stepping in, so to speak.
But now this shit is everywhere, and it feels like every ten steps a stupid sign is reminding me to go vote again, like I'm a fucking a fucking goldfish. This dog shit is everywhere.
Bob's no different from the rest of them.
But, he's different enough.
Whatever.

Don't worry, sign. I'm voting. I'm voting for me.

Thanks for the constant fucking reminder.

Even though I don't necessarily agree with the system. I'm not against voting.

Sure I could do more, but it's the least that I can do so it's a start, I guess. It bothers me how low voter turnout has been, though. Hard to support a system reliant on the people that less than half the people participate in. If all these independent people could collectively support a single independent voice within politics then maybe democracy might start working properly again.

People argue that elections are rigged and leaders are bought, but last I checked money isn't allowed to draw an 'X' beside the name of a person aiming to lead a country.

Democracy isn't necessarily broken, but the people that it depends upon arguably are. It's a shame, really. Sadly - with the way the population has become - there is no way that a single individual has any real sway among the masses, or any method of achieving the true population's support.

Great ideas - and people - are getting lost within a sea of ignorance that has more support than the islands of logic that litter it. Fuck. Wish the beer store was closer.

Stuck with my own thoughts. Trying so hard to ignore the fact that I drank piss that I'm contemplating politics.

I drank piss.

Fuck.

I need to get beer and make it to the bulrushes before dark.

I need cleansing.

Stupid fucking Bob.

"Fucking Bob. Piece of shit."

"Just let it go, Granger. It's done. He drank piss, too. It's over."

"Ha, yeah he did. He drank my piss. Hahaha, that's fucking disgusting."

"Yes. Yes, it is."

Fuck you, Nutsack. Shut the fuck up.

"Shut the fuck up. And roll up another joint, Nutsack."

"No worries. Ummm, should we get some beer soon or something? Getting to be that time."

"Well, we can just drink the rest of that bottle of Jack Daniel's. It's Bob's, fuck him."

Stupid fucking piece of shit, what are you going to do? I'm drinking your booze. Bitch.

"Whatever. Works for me. Got mix?"

Mix? Pussy. Fuck mix.

"Fuck mix."

"Hmmm, nah. I think I'd rather get some mix. At least to use as chase."

"Fucking pussy."

"Whatever, just not a fan of JD. I'm going to run across the street and grab some mix from the store. I need smokes anyway."

Ha, Nutsack's a girl.

"Go get your mix, you fucking girl."

"Whatever, man. I'll be back."

Yeah you will. Bitch.

"It doesn't matter, who is without a flaw?"

I don't get it. Whatever.

Damn. I'm full.

That was an epic meal.

This is actually quite romantic, really.

A date with Mary Jane by candlelight.

Because you're special, babe.

Szechuan chicken, sweet and sour pork, deep-fried prawns, chicken chow mein, wonton soup, almond chicken.

Almond chicken. So good, especially from this place. They do the breading just right. I hate when the breading is too thick.

That was perfect.

So full.

It's quiet here, without the hum of the fridge and whir of various electronics throughout a 'functioning' home. TV, stereo, heater, lights. None of that here.

I like it. It's peaceful.

Disgusting, but peaceful.

Fuckin' Reef. This place is far from functioning at the moment. I kinda feel bad.

Purposefully ignored my surroundings while I - while *we* ate.

It ruins the mood when I start looking around too much.

Just keep my gaze within the candlelight.

Sorry my place is such a mess, girl. It's not my fault.

The roommate, you know. He's a bit of a slob.

Reef, you really need to start picking up after yourself.

And then start picking yourself up.

Seriously. As a friend.

I guess I shouldn't say anything. I have no idea what he's going through. It's not my place to get involved and act high and mighty. Just stay out of it unless I'm asked.

What I should do is clean up a bit, though. It would probably help him out. It's okay to do that, right?

Yeah, that's a good idea.

Plus, all these long flickering shadows cast by random debris are really killing the vibe between me and my girl right now. I mean - haha - she hasn't said a word all night. I think this environment is messing with my mojo. I just wanted to spend some quality time with her - here on the couch - but I can't fully relax amongst the disorder.

The Cinderella moment is fading. The clock has struck.

These candles don't look romantic, they look cracked out.

Cracked out, unkempt, and frankly disgusting. I wouldn't go on a date with me to a place like this.

Fuck no.

Sorry, girl. I'll be right back. I need to make this place a bit more comfortable for us before we get to know each other better, if you know what I mean. Please don't leave. Just make yourself at home while I tidy up.

Seriously, though. This is bad, Reef.

You're living like a fucking squatter. It would be extremely hard to convince anyone stepping into this place that it wasn't a drug den. All it's missing are the works.

Thankfully, I know you're better than that at least.

I should really just go home, but I want to wait for him to get back. I'm not comfortable with leaving this much dope here unattended at the moment. Even though most of it's already been separated and hidden well, I still don't fully trust this place. It's not Reef's, so really we both could get barred from coming in here at any moment. I'd rather stay close to my product for now.

This place is disgusting.

Yeah, fuck it.

I'll just quickly fill a garbage back, clear off the main table, and get back to my intimate evening. I know you're getting restless, girl. I'm sorry. I'll come sit with you in a moment, almost done. I just can't get in the mood until I deal with this, you know how it is.

I wonder if he's got garbage bags around here anywhere.

Venture into the unlit caverns.

I know too much about birds. Every time I hear an unfamiliar bird song in the distance my interest is piqued and my ears perk up like an attentive predator.

Especially when it's an uncommon call.

That could have been an oriole, it's the right time of year.

It's like a 'd*oo-dee-dee-doo-dwiddly-dee'*.

I don't know. Bird calls are a hard thing to explain.

Except for the crow, I guess. Everyone recognizes a crow's *'caw'*. The chickadee is a pretty easy one to explain, too. It just goes 'c*hickadee-dee-dee'*, or sometimes 'c*heeseburger'* but usually only in the mornings for that one.

Then you have calls like the pheasant, though. Try describing that one. One of those sounds that's unmistakeable when you hear it but impossible to explain to anyone else. It's like, well, kind of like double-starting an engine with a gas tank full of tin cans.

That's as good as I can do on that one.

You have to hear it for yourself.

I can still hear that oriole behind me, and I want to turn around, find it, and identify it but I'd much rather get to the bulrushes while it's still light out.

I could go chasing birds for hours if I let myself.

But no.

Besides, the leaves are getting thick. A bit late in the season to make easy identification without binoculars. Plenty of room inside a tree to hide out of sight.

Better to go birdwatching before the trees have filled out.

I know this, from experience.

Birds. What an odd thing to be interested in. It was programmed into me as a kid, though. There are times when a flash of colour flying by will make me completely stop what I'm doing. I snap into some sort of brainwashed curiosity and I just have to find out what bird that was which flew by.

I remember staying up late reading the bird book. Studying up on species that were common in the area which I hadn't seen yet so that I could quickly identify them before they flew away.

They were birds, after all. Sometimes you'd only get a passing glance, and I wanted to be able to identify them from just that if need be.

Once you see a bird and identify it, you never forget it.

This area is almost like a tourist stop for traveling birds. Living here has always felt to me like one of those situations of 'when in Rome'. It's rather exciting if you're into that sort of thing.

The peak season is just passing.

The gathering before the migration.

For the birds, it's like driving down the highway and seeing one of the signs that a rest stop with food and shelter is up ahead, followed by a warning that the next one isn't for one hundred clicks. So you stop and rest - of course - and that's what they do.

And it draws crowds of gawkers.

People being people can't ever let nature rest peacefully. Especially when it's gathered in numbers with some celebrity species among them, so they follow.

It's a popular place for it according to enthusiasts, and the vehicles that roll through town with foreign license plates and birder bumper stickers tend to agree.

"*Caution: This vehicle stops for birds.*"

Indeed, I do.

Almost there.

It's amazing how quickly my mind starts to wander once I get close to the bulrushes. There's a calming energy here.

Almost forgot that I drank piss. Almost.

Fucking Granger.

He wasn't supposed to get involved.

It was between me and Droops.

I wonder if anyone will be out there tonight.
Doubtful, unless it's someone coming to be alone
with their thoughts
like me.

I'm fine with there being no one.

'VOTE BOB'

Strange place for one of these signs.
I should take it for kindling, though.
A fire tonight would be nice.
Good idea.
Yeah, I thought so.

I fuckin' drank piss.

Do I even really want to hang out with Granger tonight?
No. No, I don't. Who would?

Sure, there's a free bottle of booze and free tokes, but is it worth it?

The guy makes me uncomfortable, and I don't think he even really likes me. Actually, I don't think The Granger really likes anyone. He does seem to like company, though. Or more-so just likes swearing and belittling real people rather than random objects.

I should just go. This guy's a fucking idiot.

I'd like to say it's all harmless, but with him it's questionable. I can take care of myself, but sometimes would rather not be on guard all evening. And around him, I'd definitely have to stay on guard.

Uggh, yeah. I really should leave. Maybe hit up the café and see who's there.

And, wait.

Where the fuck has Spudley been this whole time?

He went for smokes and then fucked off.

Piece of shit.

I guess those Asians were looking for him, though.

Maybe he'll show up here.

Actually, I don't think he even knows Bob.

Does he?

Have they ever met? Weird.

I don't have any way to get a hold of him besides randomly wandering around, and if those Asian gangsters are still after him I doubt he'll be easy to find. Wonder what he did.

Come to think of it, that's probably why he wanted to meet up this morning. I wasn't really paying attention.

Hmmmm. Fuck.

Awkward party time with Granger, or wander randomly?

That's a tough call.

I could go out to the bulrushes, but I don't know if anyone's going to be there tonight. Plus, it's out of the way to grab beer then go out there. And there's free booze available.

Free booze. Right here.

I do like free booze.

Damn it. Looks like I'm stuck with Granger by default. Yay.

How the fuck does a person like him even function? His brain is seriously wired wrong.

It takes all kinds, I guess.

And I'm the poor bastard who is willfully choosing to hang out with him tonight.

I hope other people swing by at least, and not just casual stoners pulling an in-and-out grabbing some smoke. I hope other people actually stay and hang out. Would rather not be there alone with him drinking a bottle of the angry juice. Jack Daniel's can really bring the worst out of people.

And there's no way Bob's coming back for a while.

Fuck that.

Hahaha, he drank Granger's piss.

The saga is finally over.

Yup, Bob won't be back 'til late.

I know him well enough by now.

No doubt he's at the bar trying to wash the taste of Granger piss out of his mouth.

That's fucking gross, but that's what you get, dude.

It was coming to you.

Sorry. (Not sorry).

The phone rings for some time into his ear before someone picks it up on the other end,

"Hello?"

"Greetings. How are things going, old friend?"

"Well, well. Fancy hearing your voice. Oh, you know. They go, and I just keep getting older as they do. Same old song and dance."

"Isn't it always?"

"Indeed it is. And you know me - not complaining - just pointing out the obvious."

"Well, you never were one to complain."

"No. No, I wasn't. There are times though where maybe it would've been smarter if I would have, but what would have been the fun in that?"

They both chuckle in unison with grizzled voices.

"Well, what's putting your voice into my ear this evening, good sir?"

"I would imagine the phone itself is doing most of the work, but frankly, my words come to you because my mind figured you might be interested in a bit of youthful fun this evening. For old time's sake. You know."

"I believe I do, and will admit that I'm intrigued. I'm sure I could be coerced into partaking in some youthful fun. What seems to be the trouble?"

"No. No trouble, that would be putting far too strong of a title on the matter, and we are well beyond our years of getting involved in any real trouble. Just a situation that has presented itself that I thought you might like to enjoy remedying along my side."

"Ah. You do know I like remedying situations."

"Oh, I know you do. Which is why it would have been rude of me not to phone and offer an invite."

"Such a gentleman."

"Always."

"I definitely appreciate it, old friend. Well then, no time like the present. Is this something where I should be making haste? All I really need is to grab my coat."

"Haste isn't quite necessary, but I do agree that there is no time like the present. I'll leave the appointment in your hands. I'd never want to intrude if you had previous engagements, of course."

"No, there's no previous engagements, some youthful fun might be just what I need this evening. Yes, consider the invitation approved and warmly received. The appointment will be filled shortly."

"Excellent, I will anticipate your arrival. We can discuss it more at that time."

"Indeed. The suspense will ensure my punctuality. Until then."

"Until then. You fucking bastard."

"Now, now. I thought we were acting polite and proper. You went and broke character. Shame on you."

"Couldn't help myself. I'm in a fine mood this evening. You understand."

"Indeed, I do. Until we meet in person?"

"Of course."

With that the connection was severed.

He may not actually be the 'Lord of the Land', but he was beginning to feel quite righteous within his domain.

He chased the conversation with a glass of Glenfiddich 40 Year Old from the cabinet.

"Reef? Shit, hey. How's it going, dude?"

"Oh, hey Bob. How's it going?"

"Could be better. But nothing some beers can't fix."

"Yeah, I hear that."

Well, shit. Reef's here.

This is kind of uncomfortable. I haven't seen Reef since before the funeral, and have kind of been avoiding things since then. Well, not kind of. I've been avoiding things. Straight up. Didn't stick around for the 'after party'. Wasn't feeling festive.

"Sorry about th-"

"It's okay, man. I'd rather not talk about it."

"I get that. Sorry."

"Don't worry about it. So. What brings you here tonight?"

"Long story short? I got forced to drink Granger's piss."

"Granger? But I thought it wa-"

"Yeah, well - did you know about the beer bottle in the fridge? That one I'd been saving, from a couple weeks back?"

He's just looking at me. Piecing it all together. He knew.

"Wait, that was still there?"

"So you did know. Fuckin' Droops. Granger drank it."
"Oh, fuck! Hahaha, really?!"
"Yes. Really."
"Ha, oh shit. Wait, but it was your bee-"
"Oh, I know."
"Damn. Ha. I'm sorry, dude. What happened?"
"Fuck, I wasn't even there when it happened. I came back home to him holding a fucking broomstick ready to kill me."
"Holy shit, seriously? That guy is insane. I don't know why you ever agreed to live there."
"I don't know, either. It was a place to live, it was cheap, and I felt I could handle it."
"Yeah, but - do you still feel like you can handle it?"
"I don't know. Mostly? If that makes sense."
"Yeah. It kinda does."
"Fuck, I don't know. Right now I just want to drink some beers and forget about what happened. Still a bit too fresh in my memory."

Wow, that came across ignorant and self-centered. I hope he doesn't take it the wrong way. Wasn't thinking.

"We should probably gather up some wood for a fire before it gets too dark."
"Yeah, sorry. Didn't mean to bring it up. That's a good plan. Sucks wandering around this place in the dark."
"No, it's fine. And yeah, it does."

Thankfully, he brushed it off. I keep forgetting that he's been dealing with far more than I am lately.
It helps put my trivial bullshit in perspective, though.

Drinking piss isn't really a big deal.

"We used to kick in bathroom stalls and just beat the piss out of whoever we found inside of them. Didn't matter who the fuck it was. Hahaha, these stupid fucking pieces of shit would get their ass beat with pants down. All surprised and scared and shit."

I fucking hate this guy. Why did I decide to hang out here tonight? The free booze? Not worth it. Not right now anyway. It's sobering and tiring just listening to him talk. This guy is genuinely a piece of shit, and if I don't laugh along to his insane stories he could easily turn on me.

Fun times.

"Well, serves them right."
"I know, eh. Fuck them."

Serves them right? Thinking they can have a moment of privacy within a poorly locked public bathroom stall without someone barging in and crudely removing the teeth from their face? I'll never be able to take a shit in a public stall comfortably ever again. Those little latches do nothing.

Just a couple tiny screws and a strip of metal away from getting beat down by a stranger. Yay.

I should go. This just isn't fun.

Was a stupid idea, sticking around.

"Well, I don't know, I think I'm just going to h-"

Shit. The door flies open and my exit is ruined.

Truthfully, I'm rather thankful for the interruption.

A visitor?

Wonder who it is.

"Yo, Granger. You got that cement saw still?"
"Yeah I got it. Who wants it?"
"One-twenty good?"

"Who wants it?"
"Does it matter? One-twenty?"
"One-fifty."
"I got one-twenty."
"Fuck that I can get two bills easy for this thing. You got anything to sweeten the deal?"
"I got these pills. Ummm, how about one-twenty and – ummm - four pills?"
"Deal. Hand it over."

They do their shit and then he turns to me. I really wish it would've been a more entertaining guest.

"You wanna have some fun, Nutsack?"

Huh? Fuck. Yes. But, no.
I don't really feel like I have a choice at this point. And I really am beginning to hate being called 'Nutsack', but I suppose there isn't much I can do about it right now.
I bet he doesn't like being called 'Granger'.
Does he know we call him that?
I wonder.
As he holds a pill out in front of my face.
No. I should go.
But then I have to explain why I have to go.
Not worth the trouble.
Not the type of trouble Granger could potentially cause.
I have no exit.

"Sure, why not? What are these?"
"No clue. But here, take two."

He adds another to his palm.
This is definitely not a good idea. But I also kind of feel like I have no choice. Now I know how Bob felt. It's like he's holding out a shot glass of piss and inviting me to drink. I really shouldn't, but I know he'll get offended if I don't.

And Granger isn't fun when he's offended.

Fuck, he's just not fun in general.

Whatever. Pop the pills, chase them with some whiskey, chase the whiskey with some pop. Here we go.

Open my mouth afterwards and lift my tongue, for added presentation. Proof I actually swallowed the medicine.

"You know what, Nutsack? You're not quite a pussy after all."

Yeah? Fuck you, Granger.

I seriously hope the worst for you in life.

Just not now. While I'm here.

For now, I'll tolerate you politely.

You're just not good people. Straight up.

Fuck you.

It's weird. I can't explain why, but -

I've just always preferred smoking joints. Favourite method of inhaling, hands down. Nothing beats the feel of sitting back with a joint in hand.

I mean, I like pipes and bongs, and I've never been against doing hot knives or any other random method of smoking weed.

Except poppers. Fuck poppers.

But seriously, I could blaze for hours on end - torching bowl upon bowl of the juiciest kush, chemo, or northern lights and bubbling smoke through two, three, four chambers, whatever - but something inside me will still crave the simple satisfaction of a doobie.

It's my method of choice, and to each their own.

I've smoked through some damn impressive pieces of glass.

I've tried homemade contraptions of all shapes, sizes, and methods. You name it: Gravity tokes, second lungs, bubblers, blades, bottle tokes, vapourizers, electronic pipes, whatever. Devices made from tin cans, pop bottles, Slushee containers, vases, tubes from golf bags, Super Soaker chambers, Happy Meal toys, honey bottles, fruits, vegetables. Pipes made from nothing but cleverly folded tin foil, bongs lathed from wood. Whatever.

Just give me a classic, hand-rolled joint.

No filters, no cones or 'L-joints', Phillies, blunts, spliffs, twinkies. Coco-puffs, crosses or multi-pronged joints. Just give me the fucking original. To quote Kurt Cobain, "I will suck on the walls of her anus". I don't need to take puffs through an apple, or triple-filter my smoke through flavoured waters, or have my tokes shotgunned to me, or hot-boxed, or squeezed out of an enclosed device, or do nose hoots, or French inhales, or any of that needless shit.

A joint. A plain, old joint.

I like my ladies presented traditionally. I like to be able to hold them in my hand casually, like the way you hold a beer. I don't want instructions on where to put my fingers or provide support like it's some sort of musical instrument. Just want that natural feel, without needless effort. Nothing special. Pot smokers have a lot of creativity, but it can be put to far better use than just finding more creative ways to smoke.

It always amazes me the way a well rolled joint just burns, without any maintenance. One flick of a Bic and then the lighter can be put to rest. That cherry just quiets down when it's not being hit and then lights back up when needed. A well-rolled joint burns like nothing else.

I find a lot of people can't roll, though. Maybe that plays into it. If you can't roll, it's easy to fall back on the other methods of smoking. The crutches, if you will. I learned to roll before I even learned to smoke properly. It seemed important - like how learning to cook helps you appreciate eating - but others don't seem to see it that way. They prefer tooled methods of smoking, designed by people other than themselves. I've seen people who could easily out-smoke me, and have a far better command of their weed tolerance, but they couldn't hand-roll a joint if their life depended on it.

I hate that phrase, 'if their life depended on it', and I wish a better one came more easily to mind.

I'm baked.

But, seriously, there has to be something that makes more sense than that. Or at least something less broad. Like, I could say 'a person couldn't make a grilled cheese sandwich if their life depended upon it' but in what possibly situation would someone be holding a knife to a person's throat and forcing them to cook cheese between bread on a frying pan, or making them roll a proper joint? There has to be a better way of wording it - like - some people couldn't gain recognition for rolling a joint if there was a prize for participation.

That sucked. Rolls off the tongue terribly.

Maybe in time it will make sense.

I'm sure whoever said 'if their life depended on it' first sounded like a weirdo.

At the time.

Surely.

Phrases need to age. Yeah.

No, that was terrible. I'm just baked.

This is definitely some good weed.

"I particularly enjoy her circumference."

So baked.

Wish I could play some music inside this cave.

Music would be nice right now.

I'm still just glad this whole day turned out the way it did. I mean, it started off rough and could have ended up in a far worse place, but it didn't. It helps to have a brain sometimes.

And an ability to seize an opportunity.

And a decent grasp of people.

People...

That's the next step. I still have to flip this product.

Which reminds me, where's Reef?

That's where I'm sure he could help.

And I think that's why I'm here.

But, I've barely slept, now that I think of it.

He wouldn't mind if I napped 'til he got back.

Hey, girl. How's about we lay down for a while?

I'll take that as a 'Yes'.

The fire is going quite nicely now. And just in time.

The sun starts to dip below the bushy tips of the bulrushes and the clouds become noctilucent. Almost looks like our fire itself is what's reflecting off of the sky, but it's the light from the greenhouses causing it. I know this. They've begun covering the farm fields, and it detracts from the beauty of the moment. Eventually this place will be gone, too. Developed.

It's easy to gather up enough dead wood in the area to keep a fire going for hours. We scoured our pile from farther away, so that if we ran out there was still plenty of kindle within light of the flames.

Reef was tearing strips from a 'VOTE BOB' sign he had found somewhere, too - great minds think alike - and was slowly feeding the pieces to the fire. Like tearing strips of chicken meat for a pet, hovering around ankles at the dinner table. It burned quite well, with the heavy inks providing some green and purple to the hues.

The beers were beginning to kick in, too.

My mind began wandering curiously and I could see the

elephant's eyes glowing from the thicket.

Fuck it. I have to say something.

We've been silently staring at this fire for twenty minutes now, just thinking and smoking. I have no clue what he might be on his mind specifically, but I think I do know that he would like me to say something. I think he needs me to say something.

I have to address the eyes in the dark.

Fuck.

Alright, beers. Let's do this.

Ugghh.

Lick the salt, take the shot. Bite the lemon.

Wince.

"So. Reef. I don't really know how to say this but - you do realize you have friends, right? We're here for you. I mean, fuck. I just figure you should know that it's not like we've been avoiding you, we've just been waiting. Waiting for you. I get it. You need your time right now, but we're here. We really are, if you need someone to talk to and shit. I don't know, man. At the same time though - fuck - in all honesty, I don't know what to say. What can I say? I can't relate, and I won't fucking try to. It's not fair to you if I tried to say I knew the slightest bit about how you're feeling. You lost your Dad, man.. Shit. I don't know how to start a conversation about that. Especially if I'm not sure if you want me to. Where would I even begin? But we're not talking about anything at this point, so I guess this is what's left, eh? Not trying to pry, but I do want to show support. If you need it. Dude. Reef. You're good people. And I don't say that lightly. I hate people. You know me. Fuck. Ha, and I guess that's the point. You get me, too. Well, hopefully, I guess. And I don't normally let people get me, even if they might have a chance to. Fuck, I don't know, I'm drunk and rambling. And starting to circle talk."

Stop talking. Give him a chance to say something.

Wait for it.

Wait.

"It's okay, man. I get what you're saying. I guess, well, I don't know. I still don't know how to even talk about it properly, or articulate how I feel. It's like everything has been stirred inside me, kicked up. All this shit, all these feelings, and I'm just waiting for the layers to resettle. If that makes sense."

"Yeah I think it does, and that's fine. Just - you know - if shit starts to boil over or whatever I hope you can come talk to your friends and shit. You know, man. I'm not going to get all sappy, but I care about you, dude. Don't let your thoughts torture you from the inside out. I'm an over-thinker, I know what letting thoughts bounce around too much inside can do. It's like Pong, it'll keep gaining momentum and getting harder to deflect. Eventually, you have to let it pass by the paddle and spill into the unknown. Spill that shit if need be. If it refuses to settle. Like when you feel like you need to puke, sometimes you can calm it but sometimes it's just better to hurl."

I don't even remember what I just said.

I'm drunk and rambling, but I hope I said something that made sense. I already forgot.

Fuck.

Say something else. Damage control. Quick.

What do I say?

Reef tears more strips from the election sign.

The election...

"So who are you voting for?"

Wow, that came out far louder and sudden than I had expected. I didn't realize how long that awkward silence went for. He's looking at me quizzically.

Maybe it was actually too soon to change the subject.

"Voting for? Haven't really thought about it much, to be honest."

Really? I find that hard to believe.

You'd have to be hiding under a rock not to - oh...

"Well, maybe you should. The election's in two days."

"Two days, eh? Well, in that case, I probably won't end up voting. Not much point. So, I guess it doesn't matter who I would've chose, does it?"

"I don't know, I think it matters. If you don't vote, you have no right to complain. Right?"

"I don't have any intentions of complaining. And even if I did - sorry to say - drawing an 'X' inside of a circle doesn't really grant any sort of special entitlement or podium from which to complain from."

"Well, I don't really agree with that. I mean, I'm not a fan of the system, but it's the only one we've got and it isn't being replaced any time soon. Sorry, but it's the millions of people like you who don't see any point in taking part in the election which are causing democracy to fail right now."

"It's the millions of people like me who realize democracy wouldn't work one way or another, whether we participated or not."

"Yeah? How so?"

"Well, the way I see it the person who gets elected not only isn't chosen by the people, but rarely works for the people once chosen. We don't get to define our leader, yet he gets to define us. Doesn't seem to be much choice there."

"Of course they're chosen by the people, that's how an election works."

"Sorry, but I don't believe that's how it works at all."

"Okay. Well, let's just say - hypothetically speaking - if you were to vote for someone in two days, who would it be?"

"What does that matter?"

"What do you mean 'what does that matter'?"

"Exactly what I asked. If I don't intend to vote, what would it matter if you knew who I *would've* voted for or not? Pointless information."

"I just want to know who you would've picked."

"Why?"

"I don't know. I'm just making conversation, I guess."

"Well, fuck. It's terrible conversation."

"Sorry, but I don't get what the big deal is. So what? I asked you who you would vote for. What would that matter to me?"

"I don't know. Maybe it might affect your decision, I guess?"

"You can't affect my decision. I'm decided."

"Then why does it matter who I'd vote for?"

"I don't know. Just curious. Aren't you curious about who I would vote for?"

"Not really. Honestly I don't care one way or the oth-"

"Bob."

"I said I didn't care."

"Well then I don't care that I told you. But since I did, do you want to know why I'd vote Bob?"

"Again, no not reall-"

"Because he shouldn't win. And sometimes tossing a free coin you were given towards the underdog in the race can yield unsuspecting results."

"Unsuspecting?"

"Whatever. You know what I mean."

"I don't really think tha-"

"Indifference has never changed anything. Silence has never changed anything. In fact, it's probably prevented many things from changing."

I turned back to the fire.

He did, too.

The eyes were still there, but they dimmed.

I tried my best to ignore them.

"You're not looking so good, Nutsack."

I'm really not feeling so good either, so he's probably right. What the fuck were those pills?

They really messed me up.

Focusing is tough.

Large gaps in my thinking.

"Those...pills."

"Yeah, pretty potent shit, eh?"

His face is melting and contorting while he speaks. Colours are spilling off of him like stench lines. I don't think I should have eaten both of those pills. What were those things? His face.

Keeps bending into evil grimaces, and then when I blink,

snaps back,

and starts doing it all over again.

"I should've...only ate...one. I think."

"Nah, you'll be fine."

"What even...were those things?"

"The pills? People just call 'em 'Microdots'. I don't exactly know what's in 'em. I just know I can't stop eating 'em. Hahaha."

His laugh echoes and reverbs off of the walls of my mind. Painting colours across my vision. So many colours. I would like it a lot more if the body buzz wasn't so completely...overwhelming. Feels like I'm holding onto a jack-hammer. Slowly jarring away at my body.

But the colours...

"The...visuals."

My tongue's running through mud trying to make words happen.

"Yeah. Pretty sweet, eh? I did seven of 'em one night. Started seeing demons and goblins everywhere. Green slimy creatures with long ears and noses, and gnarly teeth and shit. Ended up beating the shit out of one of the goblins who tried to attack me. Green goo bullshit was spraying all over me and his goblin shrieks were fucking animal. It was intense. Let's do another shot."

Oh, God no. There's no way I'm drinking anymore. The thought of more booze

right now

makes my vision

spin.

I can't even find my arms.

Goblin shrieks? There's no such thing as goblins.

Wait.

Who the fuck were you beating up, Granger?

The goblin

was probably

a real person.

Uggggh, I think I need to lay down for a bit.

"Nah...no more...booze...I think I....just need to....lay down for a little while. Just until...I can see straight."

"Fucking lightweight. Whatever. Take the couch, you pussy. I'm going to keep smoking your cigarettes until you wake up."

Fucker.

Not my smokes.

No.

Stop.

I'm in no condition to stop him, though.

My guard...it has failed me.

My face. Mashed into the couch.

I'm spiraling...into...

The cat's light is fading.

Makes it feel much later than it is.

Getting pretty cold, too. Fire is shrinking.

Maybe I should go.

Before the cold starts to cut to the bone.

Still need to walk back.

Running low on beers, anyway.

` One, two, three left.

Hmmmm.

What to do.

Reef left a while ago now. I should consider doing the same.

Eventually.

I'm not ready yet.

The fire gets more mesmerizing the drunker I get.

I can't stop staring. The original form of entertainment.

Discovered by the cavemen.

Its spiked arms reaching up, glowing, and flickering away into new arms. Lost in some mystical dance.

Moving to music only it can hear.

Growing, shrinking, and twisting about.

I could stare at a fire forever.

Ever-changing, endlessly intriguing.

I wonder if there's a scientific explanation for why that is. Like a 'Moth to a Flame' theory that can equate a fire's hypnotizing quality using a rational formula. How it seems to draw out the intrigue and force an audience.

But why the intrigue?

There's no climax to the story, it burns as long as it's fed and then starves and dies. I think it has to do with the fact that the flames never seem to form the same shape twice. There are no reruns, you will never see the exact same episode twice.

Fire is infinitely unpredictable. It's hard not to stare in wonder at something that cannot be fully mapped. Its next move is always a mystery, to an extent.

Computer programs can simulate fire, but they can never properly program its methods.

The same can be said for water, I suppose. Watching a river or stream travel past, or a waterfall. I imagine it's the same sort of effect. A random pattern generator that's still reliant on basic rules and laws of nature.

Fire and water.

There must be a similar theory and formula to their intrigue.

I wonder if science has ever looked into this correlation. Attached sensors and monitors to the brains of people as they sit relaxed in front of a campfire or waterfall and respectively compared the read-outs.

I would imagine that they would find similarities.

I'd be surprised if there weren't.

This fire's starting to die, though.

I should seek out some more kindling.

Fuck, it's pretty dark, but also too early to go home still.

Fucking Granger. And fucking Droops, too.

Maybe by some stroke of luck Granger won't be there when I get back home. Not likely, though.

He will probably high as fuck, and drunker than me, and still going off about the pee bullshit.

Fuck, I hate that guy.

It's been six months of his shit now. I've had enough.

I should consider moving.

No idea where I'd go.

This fire, though.

Even though it's dying, it still looks amazing. All of the embers, breathing orange light and shining through the layers of ash. Ebb and flow of amber as air rolls across the surface.

Mesmerizing.

Whatever colour that is, I think it's my favourite. That glowing, breathing orange.

Like the tip of a lit cigarette or joint.

I should roll a joint.

Yeah, I can stay a bit longer.

The mosquitoes can feed on me for a little bit longer.

Bite longer.

Fuck it.

He bit him.

'He Who Runs The Land' fucking bit him.

The sound of Granger screaming in pain woke me out of my coma. I had never heard that sound before.

I'm still groggy from those pills but I think I can make out a couple figures across the room...

Holy fuck, that Santa Claus guy has his teeth sunk deep into The Granger's arm. I can't believe what I'm watching right now. This is insane. I'm still a bit high, but this is definitely happening right now. What. The. Fuck.

"*AAAARRRRGGGHHHHHH!* You're fucking crazy, old man!"

Yeah, this Shit Nick dude is definitely crazy. Holy shit. And he's got some Gandalf-looking fucker with him. A damn wizard.

Pinning Granger down. Knees on his shoulders.

"Hand it over, you little punk."

"Hand over the Spirit of Christmas!"

Okay, maybe I am still a little high.

"Get the fuck out of my house, you fucking geezers! Get the fuck off of me!"

This is insane.

"He's a weaselly one, eh?"
"No matter. He'll tire himself out eventually."

What the fuck is evening happening here? Is this because of Granger's comments earlier?
Damn. This landlord doesn't fuck around.

"Get off me!"
"Open your fucking hand!"
"No!"
"Open it!"

Granger wriggles an arm free and tries to take a swing at Shit Nick. Gandalf grabs his fist out of the air before it can connect and pins him back to the carpet. Shit Nick keeps struggling to release Granger's grasp, and then -

"*AAAAAARRRGGGHH!* FUUUCCK! WHAT THE FUCK?!"

He fucking bit him again! Fucking Santa's a cannibal beast!
Fuck. This is crazy. These two seniors are just completely owning Granger. There's no way he's winning this one. It's not stopping the crazy bastard from trying, though.

"Open your hand and give me the damn piece of paper. You've lost. Stop behaving like an animal. This is getting pathetic."
"Fuck you!"
"Yes, fuck me. You really should work on your vocabulary, boy."

Santa lands a couple solid blows across Granger's ugly-ass

face. Fuck, just give them what's in your hand, dude.

It's over. You're done.

"Give me the damn receipt!"

"No! Get out of my house!"

"Boy, as soon as that piece of paper is pulled out of your pathetic hand this won't be your home anymore. Does that frighten you? You look a bit frightened."

"Get the fuck off me!"

"Not much depth to this one, eh. I'm getting impatient."

"Fuck you, too! Fucking Gandalf, fuck."

"Have you had your fun yet? Can we just end this already?"

"If you insist."

"*AAAAAAAAAAHHH!!!!* DAMN IT! FUCK YOU! FUCK YOU!"

Santa bit in much deeper that time, and Granger's hand quickly flowered open, revealing the rent receipt they were after.

He pulls his head back and there's smears of blood across his pure white beard. Blood starts to pour from the wound in Granger's arm and he pulls the receipt from his weakened grasp.

"FUCK YOU! FUCK YOU! FUCK YOU! FUCK YOU!"

"Got it."

These guys are fucking psycho.

Wait. What about me?

What are they going to do about me laying here?

WhatdoIdowhatdoIdowhatdoIdowhatdoIdo?

"Well, I'll admit. That was kind of fun. Definitely been a while."

"FUCK YOU! GIVE IT BACK! FUCKING GIVE IT BACK NOW!"

"Definitely. You mind if I shut him up now?"

"FUCK YOU! FUCK YOU FUCKING PIECE OF SHIT! FUCKI-"

"Please, do."

One punch.

Gandalf twisted his frame while still positioned on his knees and struck a blow across Granger's temple that knocked him out cold. Fuck.

They kept his limp body pinned to the ground for a couple more minutes while they laughed.

They were seriously having fun right now. What the fuck?

Who the fuck are these guys? I knew that Santa dude was creepy, but I didn't expect him to be this fucking sadistic. What do I do? Just keep laying here pretending to be asleep? I doubt th-

"So what should we do about this one?"

"Who? The kid pretending to sleep on the couch?"

...oh, fuck.

"He's not a problem. Right? Hey, you!"

Me? Of course he means me.

"You, there on the couch. I know you can hear me."

"Yeah?"

"You know who I am, right?"

"Yeah. Ummm, you're the guy who runs the land."

"Yes, that's right. You have a good memory. I have a couple things to add to it, if you don't mind?"

"Uh, yeah sure?"

"Excellent. Well, you can tell your other friend - Bob is it? - that he's still safe here and welcome to stay if he likes. I'm sure he will. We'll take care of removing this trash here, and tomorrow I will come back with a truck for his unwanted things. You won't have to worry about this rodent ever coming back. I take pest control quite seriously. Trust me."

"Ummm, okay."

"Okay, indeed. Consider this issue resolved, and when I come tomorrow I will have a new rent receipt made up in your friend's name."

He's being polite, but there's still blood in his beard.

They pick Granger up by his arms and legs and 'remove' him with ease, like they've done this sort of thing before.

I think I'm completely sober now.

What the...?

What the fuck is that noise?

There's somebody climbing in the fucking window!

Oh, right. It's probably just Reef.

Must've dozed off for a bit there.

Wonder how long I was out.

There's no sense of time in this place. He seriously needs to get a clock or something.

The candles still have a bit of length to them.

Couldn't have been that long.

Still, I shouldn't have passed out with all these candles lit.

Fuck, how long was I out?

"Oh, hey. You're still here?"

"Yeah, sorry. Was waiting for you to get back. Kinda passed out."

"Shit, you cleaned up? You didn't have to do that, dude."

"Don't worry about it. The least I could do for letting me hole up here while I get shit figured out."

"Oh, right. Your stuff. So, how did that go? Did you get shit figured out?"

"Got a joint rolled, waiting to tell the story. You ready for this shit?"

"Fuck yeah I am. Spark it up."

"Sweet. Okay. So basically, they found me no problem once I went out wandering around, and they take me to bossman's house. He just lives with his girlfriend - or whatever - but that doesn't matter. Anyway, he's all like:

'Spudley, let's talk.'

And I'm like:

'Yes. Let's.'

Thoughts are already spinning through my head of all the different things he could say next. All the different ways he could attack me and how I might have to defend myself, right?

And he just goes:

'I'll cut to the chase. Do you have something of mine?'

Bam. Just like that.

Okay. Okay, so I have this planned, so I say:

'Yeah. I do.'

And he just stares me down. Just fucking staring at me. I can see him starting to get mad, and looking at me like I'm an idiot-thief-rat-bastard, right?

And the he just calmly starts going:

'Well, that was easy. What did y-'

And I can hear his voice starting to rise, right?

And so I decide to just cut in with:

'I brought it with me. Do you want it? Here.'

And I jump right to the next step. I throw him a curve ball and put a small bag of weed on the table before anything could get carried away.

I could see it confused him a bit. I mean, who would expect a person to admit guilt - with what's on the line - and then pull out such an insignificant and innocent piece of pilfering?

I mean, it was like thirty bucks worth of weed I laid out in front of him in this sad, crumpled up sandwich baggie. I'll admit, I was proud of myself at that moment - the plan was working - and I started getting a bit confident. So he just looks at it for a while. Stares at the little fucking baggie, right?

And then finally says:

'What's this?'

So I put on a bit of the innocent-puppy-eye thing and I look him dead on - as honestly as I possibly can - and I go:

'This is what I have. Of yours. I've smoked a couple joints, though. I apologize, I th-'

And that's where he stood up and cut me off, and I thought I was a dead man. I seriously thought he was going to blurt out with something like:

'What sort of a fucking idiot do you take me for? Do you think you can walk in here and pull the puppy eye thing on me after stealing my shit and get away with it?'

You know, the whole, 'I invented the puppy eye!' thing. And 'You're not fooling anybody, punk!' No, instead he goes:

'Is this a joke? This is like, an eighth of weed.'

If he would have only said the first part, I may have abandoned ship, and gone with one of the lifeboats I had prepared, in case all my over-thinking was simply that and my plan was full of holes.

But, it sounded like he was buying it. It sounded like he was buying the innocent and loyal minion act that I was hoping to portray, and so I went with it. I kept going. I said:

'No. I'm dead serious,'

And I stuck to it. I was like:

'I knew I'd be seeing you today, so didn't think I needed to take any more. I've smoked a few, and I figured we would work out whatever I've smoked from what I'm owed for the delivery.'

Or whatever - you know, something like that - and just started rambling on. Repeat confess my simple crime, and overplay its significance - pretty much waiting for him to stop me - until he jumped in and was like:

'There's no way you smoked a half a pound of my fucking weed.'

Hahaha, that's seriously what he said.

It took me a moment to get it, but once I did, I realized that he was totally buying the innocent dumb routine. So, I guess maybe a bit pretentiously I was like:

'Excuse me? No. There's definitely no way that I could have.'

So he's like:

'Well, then where the fuck is my weed? Are you fucking with me, Spudley? Don't try and fuck with me.'

So, now I could see he was getting frustrated and shit, right? But basically, I know I'm off the hook. Now I'm not a suspect, his brain is just starting to hurt a bit from thinking about who the next most likely suspect is. So, bam, I start going into phase two, and planting the seed, and keep him talking so I go:

'I'm sorry. I'm definitely not fucking with you. I'm not lying. I apologize.'

And he stops for a moment, looks up at me, and I can see he's starting to think about it differently, and he goes:

'Then where is my weed?'

And he sits back down.

And I'm thinking in my head, 'Close, but you're still not asking the right questions.' But I can't say that right? So I answer him honestly - because that's all I can do at this point - and I say:

'I don't know.'

And he stops again.

And again, I can see him thinking about it.

Thinking about what to say next, and then he strikes closer.

He points at me and goes:

'But, you know something.'

Right? And I have to give him that one. So I'm like:

'Well, yeah. Maybe I do know something.'

Maybe too soon. Maybe it was too soon for that line, but I felt like we might have beaten around the bush for a while if we didn't. So he yells back at me:

'Well, fuck! What do you know?'

And I say:

'All I can do is tell you what happened last night.'

And then he cuts me off and starts going off about something or another like:

'I don't care about the cops and the drop and all that, I just want to know blah-blah-blah.'

So, I cut him off, jump in, and just just go:

'I know. All I can tell you is what happened once we were back at the house. After the weed was taken out of the car. Can you just listen? I'll tell you.'

I don't think he was expecting that, and that was what I was hoping, right? So anyway, he goes:

'Okay. What happened at the house?'

So I told him.

I told him about how there was a guy sneaking into the room and scooping handfuls of weed out of the package and leaving.

I told him that I didn't want to be caught up in that situation, so I took a little bit of weed to smoke knowing I'd see him soon because I'm still owed my cut from the delivery, and that I went home. I was tired. I went the fuck home.

And then I told him that I really enjoyed the weed that I smoked, and thought that I could probably sell it.

Since I wasn't comfortable driving the drops anymore.

You know.

So...

That's how I now have two quarter pounds instead of one, five hundred bucks, and this fancy new digital scale to keep track of what I have."

Pull the weed from under the table for the grand reveal.

Bam.

I was waiting far too long to tell that story - getting anxious - but I think I still did it justice.

"Dude! Nice. Well played."

"Thank you. I thought you'd appreciate the story. And hey, I appreciate the hospitality. So. Let's smoke another one, and then figure things out in the morning? I need to line up some buyers. It's cool if I crash here tonight, right?"

"Yeah, no worries. I'm down. And as for a plan, I may be a step ahead of you."

"That's what I like to hear. Roll it up."

"Time to wake up."

"What the...ugggh..."

"Wakey wakey. Hey, kid. Wake up. Time to get out of the car."

"What the fuck? Where did you guys take m-"

"Don't worry, you're fine. We just had to remove you from my property because you were trespassing, see? You had no reason to be on my property. So I had to -"

"Fuck you, trespassi-"

"So I had to remove you."

"I fucking paid my rent you fucki-"

"No. See, you didn't. I don't have anything that shows you were renting that property, do you? I didn't think so. So this is what is going to happ-"

"What about all my fucking stu-"

"This is what is going to happen. Animals don't get stuff, and since you chose to behave like an animal then you will be treated as such. But, I'm a fair man, and objects do have value so I will give you one hundred dollars, which I th-"

"You fucki-"

"Which I think is more than reasonable. Considering the damage you have done to my property when you entered it illegally."

"I didn't fucki-"

"So what I suggest you do, is take this bit of fortu-"

"I fucking sugges-"

"Is take this bit of fortune, and start rebuilding yourself back up from an animal into a man again. My friend Gandalf here - as you so colourfully named him - will now be renting that basement suite. I believe I will be staying with him for a few days as well, to redecorate, and greet any visitors that may swing by so that I can inform them that visitors are no longer welcome."

"You fucki-"

"I strongly suggest you take this offer, and leave the vehicle quietly. You have no grounds from which to negotiate any alternative. I can assure you of this."

There's a moment of silence.
Enough to hear the breeze swim through the night.

"Ah, you're actually thinking before speaking. Excellent. Maybe you're beginning to understand the reality of the situation you're in."

"Fine. Give me the money. But this isn't over."

"I think you'll find that it very much is."

Granger grabs the money and exits the vehicle mumbling.
Under his breath.

Defeated.

"There you are. Where the fuck have you been dude?"

"Out at the bulrushes drinking. Ran into Reef. Granger here?"

"Nope. Gone."

"Good. Hopefully he doesn't bother coming back tonight. Fucking piss. Piece of shit. Thanks for having my back on that one. Fucker."

"Hey, you had it coming to you. At least now we're even."

"Yeah, but I had to drink Granger piss."

"Haha. Yeah you did. That's fucking disgusting. I'd never drink Granger piss. Want some whiskey?"

"Fuck you. Wait, did you guys drink most of my whiskey? What the fuck?"

"Don't worry about that. Listen to me, Granger's gone. So,

look at the big picture here. You won't ever have to deal with Granger again."

"He'll be home eventually."

"No he won't. Not this time. That's what I'm trying to tell you. Plus, I bet he has some weed still in the freezer. I'll grab a sack and roll one up. That weed's yours now too, dude."

"I don't get it. Cops come and grab him or something? Finally. Fuck. I'm taking a smoke."

"No worries. And nope, it was a forceful eviction."

"Forceful eviction?"

"Yup. Seriously. It was fucking crazy. You should've fucking seen it. But you're good, though. That's the point. That Santa Claus dude says he likes you, just hates Granger."

"Wait, what the he-"

"Okay. Sorry, I'm still a bit high. I'll try to slow down a bit. See, they got in an argument earlier, right? And the landlord guy was all super calm about it and just left, but then he came back later with this Gandalf fucker and they booted him the fuck out. Like, booted him the fuck out, dude. You should've seen it. It would've made up for drinking his piss. I mean, that Santa dude bit him - but anyway, yeah, I guess this is your place now."

Holy shit. He's gone.

He's finally fucking gone.

This feels like a dream. I almost want to do a victory lap around the property. Can I? I guess there's no one to stop me.

Six fucking months of his crazy, but I finally earned my prize.

This place is mine now.

Patience pays off, sometimes.

I feel like a giant at the moment.

Damn. This is going to take a while to sink in.

I actually have this place all to myself now. I almost want to kick Droops out and march around naked.

Victoriously strutting, and letting my cock out to survey its new kingdom.

'Yes, my cock. This filthy kitchen, and these piles of crusty

dishes and beer cans belong to us now. This tattered couch is ours as well. Everything within these basement walls is ours to command. Behold.'

This kingdom is in a state of ruin.

The years spent under the cruel hand of Granger The Stranger have taken their toll, and will forever be remembered as dark times. But now we enter a new age.

The age of Bob.

It will take time, but we will rebuild.

"We have the technology...we can rebuild him."

And I have the desire.

I do really like this place, and I'll wear my crown of thorns upon this pile of shit. It's a dump, but I'm not fancy, and I detest opulence. This place is functional. Or, it will be.

It can be.

Mostly.

"Alright, dude. Joint's rolled. You spark it, in honour of your new place. Like a smudging."

"Nah, man. Roller's rights. And, so - the piss saga is done? We good?"

"We good."

He's gone. He's fucking gone.

Fuck you, Granger. Fuck.

I wonder what's going to happen to his shit.

Do I have to deal with it?

And how much weed did he leave in the freezer?

I should go look...

"And what do you suppose we have here, I wonder?"

No, I can wait. Droops knows what's in there.

I still don't fully believe it, though.

Granger can't be gone.

This seems too easy.

Waking up to a cement saw, and drinking your roommate's piss is easy?

Maybe this is really over.

"Give me another one of these."

"Yeah sorry, buddy. Closing soon. I think it's about time you settled up your tab."

"I'll settle up my tab when I'm done fucking drinking."

"Well, you're done drinking. So how about you settle up your fucking tab?"

Who the fuck does this guy think he is?

I'll tell him when I'm done drinking.

"I'll fucking tell you when I'm done drinki-"

"No, actually. I'll fucking tell you. And you're done drinking."

Excuse me?

"Excuse me?"

"You have a hearing problem or something? I said time to pay up."

Pay up. I'll fuckin' tell you when I'm ready fuckin -

"Listen. I'll fucking tell you when I'm ready to pay up. Just give me two more of these -"

"No. You're fucking cut off, buddy. Pay your fucking tab and get the hell out of here."

"You pay your fucking tab."

"Pay my- What? Seriously?"

Yeah, seriously. Bitch.

"Yeah, seriously. Bitch."

"Really, guy? Fuck this. I don't have time for this shit."

Well, I don't have time for your shit. Walk away, faggot.

"Well, I don't have time for your shit. Walk away, faggot."

"Whatever, dude. Hey, Fecma! Hey! You want to deal with this piece of shit for me? Here's his bill. Yeah, that dude there. I've got customers lining up, and this guy wants to act tough and shit. Big man over here. Just call the fucking cops when you're done."

Calling in backup. Pussy.

Oh, so now this long-haired fucker wants to have a go, eh?

Let's do this, bitch.

"Now I lay me down to sleep, I pray the Lord my soul to keep. And if I die before I wake, I pray the Lord my soul to take."

Haha, weird. I still can't help but think of that.

I guess being raised Roman Catholic, every now and then this little lullaby still pops in my head when I'm falling asleep.

So creepy. If you think about it.

I mean, fuck that, 'when the bow breaks the cradle will fall' bullshit. It's got nothing on religious lullabys. Not nearly as fucked up as willfully giving your soul to an unknown entity if he should choose to take it during the night.

Like, wait. Wait a second. Why would I die before I wake?

Back this 'Smells Like Children' carriage up a second.

If I die before I wake?

I was a kid. I didn't know that was an option. Didn't think children died in their sleep often enough to warrant that prayer every night. I think I may have even learned about death for the first time through that little rhyme, or questioned what it was at least. But they make it sound like it's a good thing.

All children come unto the Lord right? This is seen as a positive message to children. As a somewhat adult person now, that shit is straight fucked up.

Seriously.

One thing I will give the Bible credit for - which it would oddly denounce if offered an award for - is the way it acknowledges spirituality, the afterlife, and the concept that our energy is eternal. Those are some heavy ideas, hidden within stories and fairy tales.

Kudos on that one.

But, beyond the deep and meaningful messages these stories contain, everything else is just fluff.

Clever, believable fluff, but fluff nonetheless.

I remember questioning the Bible once to my Dad when I was a kid, and wondering how he could possibly believe that the world was created in seven days - him being a logical man - and he surprised me with his logical answer.

He told me that of course the world wasn't created in seven days. It didn't happen over the course of Monday, Tuesday Wednesday, etc. and it didn't occur during seven revolutions of the earth. What must have occurred though, were those steps.

In that order.

That makes sense.

So why the seven days of creation?

Well, how do you possibly explain the creation of the universe to a vast amount of people as best as possible when the majority of the population is uneducated? You simplify it, and you keep simplifying it so that even if it is the first book you learn how to read, you can visualize and interpret the ideas within.

Sadly, these ideas have been tampered with by lesser minds with ill-intent over the years, and the text in general can't be trusted, but the ideas remain.

The core concept is that there are spiritual beings, other-worldly beings. Life beyond this realm is held dear to religion.

So with that, I would have to give it merit. Religion opened my mind at a young age to what might be beyond those ideas.

Wondering what might happen if I actually died.

Died before I woke.

I still wonder.

I guess it could still happen.

If Granger comes back while I'm unconscious.

"I must say, that was quite fun."

"Indeed. And it has definitely been too long since we've partaken in such an eventful evening."

"Undoubtedly. But anyways, let's cut the bullshit, Nick. What's with scaring the shit out of those little punks?"

"Well, that ugly fucker needed to be taught a lesson in respect, basically. He was causing unneeded attention."

"Ah, I see. And you felt the need to bite him?"

"He felt the need to try swinging kicks towards my twig and berries, so fuck yeah. I had no problems biting him."

"Fair enough. He was quite the squirmy worm. And the other one who lives there? The roommate?"

"I don't know who the kid on the couch was, but Bob, I like him. He understands respect."

"Fair enough."

"Fuck, those kids' weed looked like shit. Eh?"

"Ha. Indeed it did. Trimmed by amateurs, and the grow looked rushed, even from a quick glance. I imagine the ash isn't too clean. This on the other hand, this is some tasty smoke. Thanks again for the invite, I needed that."

"Anytime, old friend. Anytime."

The cameras pan away from the landlord's house, up through the roof revealing Bob's new kingdom across the street, where we quickly x-ray inside - through the upstairs neighbour's domain - and see Bob taking comfort in his bed, and Droops still fondling roaches upon the couch. Clip to Spudley and Reef, sleeping around the last candle that's still lit in the powerless suite. And somewhere in the distance, the sound of sirens and the flash of cherries become more apparent, as they roll through town to pick up Granger from outside the Village Pub, where he's bloodied and broke.

End scene.

Fuckin' piece of shit tried scratching my eyeball.

Fuck.

Cops can have fun with that one, fuckin' piece of shit.

I hope I get a decent cut out of his wallet.

And cut your fucking nails, dude. Seriously.

Fuck. Oh, well.

Hopefully it was worth it.

"Exit light. Enter night."

"What did he owe?"

"Forty-five fifty."

Hundred in his wallet. Not bad.

Over fifty bucks for a couple cat scratches and a fun story to tell Bob next time I see him, definitely worth it.

Granger isn't having a good night.

"Well, here you go. With tip. And this should cover my tab."

"Sweet, thanks."

"No, thank you. Mind if I grab one more? I know that guy, actually. And if the cops do what they should with him it would mean good fucking fortune for an old friend."

"Yeah, man. Don't worry about it. This one's on the house."

Yeah, one last beer then I'll head upstairs, I guess.

I'm sure the hallways will be rowdy at this hour.

Maybe I'll get to bounce another idiot.

Nah, fuck that. Too much effort.

I should crash.

Besides, I think those pills Dave gave me are wearing off.

The bar's looking dull again.

"Okay! Everybody out! That's it. Bar's closed. Go the fuck home! You may not be wanted there, but you're not wanted here anymore either. Sorry, folks. Everyone out."

Yeah everyone. Go the fuck home.

I am home.

This is my living room.

Sleep is starting to call my name, though.

Cherries breathe through the bar windows.

"Take my hand..."

Time to climb the stairs to slumber.

"...off to never never land."

FADE TO BLACK.

"We are now one day away from electing a new governing party in this country, and on the eve of this election we will be maintaining constant, in depth coverage, bringing you up to date information on this final leg of the race. Even at this point, analysts are still hesitant to predict a clear winner with most looking at the 'Vote Bob' campaign as an unpredictable wild card. So, what do you think about this? Do you honestly believe that their fringe party can win, or even achieve the role of opposition?"

"The problem for me is not the matter if they *can* win, but if they should be *allowed* to win if the numbers do in fact give them control of the House."

"I don't understand what you mean."

"Well, we don't know anything about what these people stand for. What is their platform? You have a simply absurd campaign structure built around a mystery and aiming to elect an anonymous figurehead. They're making a mockery of the system, and of democracy itself. It shouldn't be allowed."

"I understand what you're saying, but their party members are not necessarily anonymous. If their party were to win the election, they are within their rights to choose at that time which amongst them would serve as Prime Minister. Any party has the right to do this. Despite your personal objections, the courts have looked into their campaign, and everything they are doing is considered acceptable under the laws governing elections."

"Barely, and it's a disgrace. 'Vote Bob'. What are you voting for if you vote for Bob? Nobody knows. At this point, I can only base my assumptions on the fact that the citizens of this country won't buy into a gimmick when choosing their leader and will stick to the established political candidates. There is no possible way that this Bob character could win a majority vote."

"But what if he does? What do you think that sort of outcome would mean for the people of this country?"

"Well, I don't really want to think of that possibility. Holding a majority government in this country grants you a lot of freedoms regarding the structure - and restructuring - of laws within these borders. It could be catastrophic to give that sort of power to a nascent political party with no credible political experience, whatsoever."

"Some have argued though, that political experience hasn't really gotten us very far these past couple decades and would cite low voter turnout as proof that maybe the system could use a bit of shaking up. Fresh blood. What would you say to those people?"

"I would say give your head a shake and go read a book."

"Very well. On that note, let's go over to Lisa and take a look at our weather forecast for the rest of the week. Lisa?"

"Hello?"

Morning?

Morning.
Actually, it's probably afternoon by now.

"...stick my head under the pillow"

Feels nice to sleep in. Such crazy dreams.
I should probably get up, though.

"Droops? You still here?"

I yell from my bed towards the living room - a wall and a door frame separate the two areas - and he quickly responds over the music.

"Ah, you're alive. Yeah, man. I'll roll one up."

"Cool shit. What time is it? Had the weirdest dream."

"Almost 2 o'clock. Weird dream? What was it?"

"No clue. Forgot it already, I just remember it feeling very strange."

"It's so groovy when I'm dead."

What was it? The memory is fading fast.

It was one of those long adventure dreams that seem real, but my mind can't latch on to any details of it anymore.

I think I remember a river.

No matter. Today's a good day.

The first day of a Granger-free life.

I still get this feeling like he's not exactly gone, though.

"The phone it rings and it's the landlord.
The door it knocks and it's the-"

*** KNOCK, KNOCK KNOCK ***

Oh, fuck.

Fuck, fuck, fuck. There's someone at the door.

"Who is it?"

"Ha. You scared it's Granger?"

"No. Just, who the fuck is it?"

"It's not Granger, dude."

"I know. Just - go check!"

"I'm checking... It's your landlord. The Santa Claus one."

"Ummm, I guess let him in?"

Right, Droops said that he would be back today.

For some reason, I actually was a bit worried it would be Granger. Problems like him usually don't go away so easily.

I should know better, though.

Granger would never knock.

He would be more likely to hack the door down with an axe.

With a big ole '*Heeeeere's Granger!'*

"It's so groovy when I'm deeeeeeeaaaaad."

Quickly throw on some pants, find my hat, and walk out into the living room. The old man is already standing there. He's so hard to get a proper read on. Calm and collected. A sharp mind hiding within the frame of an innocent old man.

"I'm here to - do you mind turning that down?"

"Oh, sorry."

"Thank you. Anyway, I'm here to dispose of your buddy's possessions. Anything you don't want, of course."

"Granger? Yeah, his stuff is all in that room - or area - I guess. But, I don't really underst-"

"Listen, I've got no problem with you. I can work with you. You seem like a solid kid, but that other guy proved himself to be disrespectful. In my opinion, that puts him amongst the animals, and animals don't get to live indoors unless they are welcome as pets. As you know, I don't allow pets here."

I'm not sure if that was supposed to be funny.

"With that being said, I have a truck parked in the driveway, and you're welcome to load it up with anything you would like taken to the dump. I won't help you load it, but I'll gladly remove the refuse and dispose of it once you are finished."

"Okay, but what abou-"

"I'll give you about an hour to fill it up, however you like. Oh, and as for Mr. Granger. Word came through the scanner last night that he was picked up after an incident at the bar around closing time. As it turns out he fit the description of a break and enter suspect, also wanted on assault charges. So, safe to say he's going to have his hands full for a while. I'll be sure to let you know if the situation changes, though. I figured you would like to know."

This is all so confusing, I just have to ask.

"Why're you being so nice to me?"

"Why? Let's just say I see everything that happens around here. You've been here six months now, so it's safe to say that I've gotten a good feel for your character, and the ones around you. That Granger fellow was cramping your style, but I imagine you were biding your time and being patient until he inevitably wound up in jail. Let's just say I was getting impatient, too. So I helped speed up the process."

"Well, thank you?"

"No worries, I'll be back in an hour to pick up the truck, and I'll leave the adjusted rent receipt for the month in your mailbox. Cheers."

Hmmm. Interesting.

That guy actually seems like a good person to have on my side. And I think I'm going to do my best to keep it that way.

He lets himself out as if he owns the place.

Which he does.

I've never been a big fan of coffee.

It doesn't seem like Reef is either by the way he's ignoring the mug and preferring to stare out the café window.

Obviously deep in thought.

Wonder what he's thinking about.

This place is dead. There's a light rain, but seriously, it shouldn't be enough to stop people from going out. What day of the week is it? Monday? That would explain it.

"Is it Monday today?"

"All day, unless it rains."

"Really? Well, it's raining."

"Sorry, just an expression my Dad used to use. Never quite understood it."

"Yeah, I think that line's only supposed to be used on Sundays."

"Hmmmm. Makes sense."

His gaze never left the street. Maybe he was looking at me through the faint reflection in the glass. There isn't enough detail to tell.

"You were up and out the window early this morning."

"Huh? Yeah, I had to go pick up my car. Plus, an idea got put into my head last night at the bulrushes and I felt like doing a bit of research."

"Research?"

"Yeah, I went to the library for a while. Used the computers."

"Odd."

That word broke his gaze. He turns to me and I can tell he's in a pretty serious place at the moment. He's not just deep in thought, he's somewhere near thought bottom.

"Maybe for you."

He notices his coffee and takes a sip - dramatically - before finishing his sentence.

"But I like going to the library. Haven't been there in a while. It's relaxing."

"Alright, fair enough. The library's cool. I'm a square. So, what did you find out about?"

"Not quite sure really, but I'm getting extremely curious about this election."

I give him a moment to elaborate, but he doesn't. Maybe he was expecting me to pry. He eventually returns to looking out the window. Fun stuff. I'm bored.

Maybe I should head home. Haven't been there in a while.

Right, we were supposed to go meet someone.

"Anyway, who was it you wanted me to meet? Some Bob guy?"

"Bob? Oh, that Bob. Right, sorry. Yeah. Well, his roommate Granger would be the one with the money. But yeah, he might be interested in some quantity if the price is right. Okay, let's go there. Yeah. I warn you, though. Granger's a bit of a psycho, but Bob's cool shit."

Pot sales and psychos.

Now this sounds far more interesting than silent coffees in a dead café.

"Alright, let's finish up these coffees and do this."

I'm ready for a bit of excitement.

"Taken by surprise, by the size of my brain
Knowing all the time, all the lies, all the games.
Thinking up a storm, when it storms it's going to rain.
Taking what's mine, all the time. All the time."

This kingdom is mine now.

You never really know how bad things are until you start working on improving. I've been living like this for six months. Six months of never being able to cook in Granger's disgusting kitchen, or sit at the kitchen table, which is a monument of garbage swarming with insect followers.

Was it this bad when I moved in?

The ensuite washer and dryer are buried beneath a mountain

of dirty clothes.

Just keep filling garbage bags, carry them up the stairs, and load them in the truck.

Where I lived controlled me.

Now it's time to control where I live.

Lay claim.

It's like waking up from hibernation.

The windows had been drawn shut since I moved in and when I crack them open to get a bit of air down here it rushes in with a desperate urgency. I wonder if there's a vacuum hiding in this mess somewhere. Still nowhere near that point, but I feel surprisingly motivated.

It's a rare feeling.

And so is being able to listen to my own music. I had gotten used to drowning out the three or four albums that Granger listened to on repeat, or thought I had, until my ears opened back up to some real music.

Fuck yeah. I feel good. This calls for a celebration.

I mean, I've spent so long living in anticipation of this moment I don't quite know what to do now that it's here. I do know that I'm going to make this place comfortable again, and less like a cave.

Once I'm done clearing out all the garbage and worthless shit I'll just move everything left from my old closet of a room into Granger's larger space.

Yeah, this area could almost be considered a real room. If it had a door. His nasty futon can go in my old room, I'll keep the lamp and night stand, probably chuck out the rest of what's in here. Junk. So much junk.

This place has opened up quite a bit already, for now I'll just finish loading the truck before it's gone and worry about interior design later. Besides, I'm going to need a smoke break, to sit back and think about it properly. Assess the area and plot things out in my mind before I go moving shit around randomly.

Work smart, not hard.

And think baked, not sober.

"...the window will shine a light on what's left for me."

"I want to stop somewhere first before we go to Bob's."

"Yeah, no worries. Where we going?"

"You'll see."

Reef took a left turn, and began winding through a suburban neighbourhood. After a maze of lefts and rights, down lanes and crescents and drives of identical houses we reached the back end of the community, which opened up into farmland. He stopped the car, lit a cigarette, and got to know it a bit before speaking.

"Okay, so. How do I put this? See that car right there?"

"What car?"

"That car. The blue Audi, sitting in the driveway."

"What car? What driveway?"

"That car. Right there."

"I don't see a car, dude. It's just a farm field. What's your point?"

"You don't see the house? The one-story rancher? With a horseshoe, gravel driveway and an Audi parked in front of the two car garage?"

"Nah, man. Am I supposed to?"

"I don't know, are you?"

"I don't fucking know, man. What're you talking about?"

"Well, this house here, and car, and driveway, that you don't see, belong to Robert Blytheswood."

"Sure. And who the hell is Robert Blytheswood?"

"He's Bob. Bob Blytheswood. The Bob seeking election in our municipality, and this is where he lives."

"But there's nothing here."

"Are you sure?"

"Okay. I'm confused."

"I was too when I came here this morning after grabbing the car. I didn't know what I expected to find, but I didn't think I'd find this."

"I still don't get it. So, do you see a house?"

"Of course not. But according to this picture here that I printed out at the library..."

He reached into his pocket and pulled out a piece of paper folder in quarters. It was an image of a one-story rancher, with a blue Audi parked out front a two car garage. Along a horseshoe driveway.

"This is what his house looks like. And according to my research, this is where the house should be."

"But it's not."

"No, it's not. 13461 Fletcher Drive. And don't even bother asking me how I found this road, which also doesn't exist. It's not scheduled to be constructed for another six months, at least."

"So..."

"So, I started digging deeper. Trying to find any physical evidence of Robert Blytheswood."

"And?"

"Nothing."

"What do you mean nothing?"

"I mean exactly that. Work, home, family, hobbies, everything was a dead end. Just like this street here, and the house there. In conclusion, I'm not sure if Mr. Blytheswood exists."

"That's fucked up."

I'm trying to think what this all means, but I can't seem to put it together.

"So what does it mean?"

"I don't really know yet, but after hitting a series of dead ends here, I started looking into other municipalities."

"Okay, and? Same thing?"

"So far. Granted, it's been harder to get the information I'm looking for the further outwards I look, but even still I haven't found a single bit of evidence that any of the people running in this 'Bob' party exist."

"Hmmmm. That's really strange."

"Yup."

Reef is still staring out over the field as if he thinks a house may yet materialize at the given address, then butts out his cigarette and looks over at me,

"Know what else?"

"What?"

"They're all named Bob. Every single person running in a municipality - all across the country - is named Bob. Some were born Roberts, but they're all running as Bobs."

"So, they're trying to rig the election?"

"No. I don't think that's what it is. You rig an election from behind the scenes, not in plain sight, and as far as I'm concerned elections have been rigged since long before we were born. No, this is something different. It's almost like a marketing campaign, and 'Bob' is their mascot. A carefully chosen archetype."

"But isn't that what all elections are? Marketing campaigns to elect their mascot?"

"Yes, but... Hmmmm, how do I put it? Well, think of it this way, sure it's still the same thing really. The difference is that by using this sort of angle all the roles that are usually necessary for a successful campaign aren't being filled by actual, *real* people.

"Before, you still had to have real people - and scores of volunteers - with the inherent flaws that come with being a real human being. Under that sort of system, it's easier to judge the individual person, compare them to the other candidates, and really localize your perspective on the big picture. You have a face to the name, so to speak. You can put each candidate under the microscope and search for kinks in their armour.

"But Bob is only real enough to be voted for, not nearly real enough to be examined. Before, they wanted to sell you on the idea that the man getting elected is the same man you saw giving donations to food banks and holding babies, not the one involved in political bribery and marital affairs. This Bob campaign has taken the human element completely out of the equation. It's a fascinating loophole, really. Bob can't be seen as doing anything wrong because no matter how you look at it, Bob's not doing anything, so it can't be wrong.

"Now picture this one entity known as Bob - which can't be wrong - up against an army of opposition. Every last soldier up against him has the 'potential' of being wrong, simply by being a physical, human opponent. Does that sort of make sense? It's like saying that Ronald McDonald is never wrong or responsible because he lacks that human element, but if you replace Ronald with a human face, like the actual CEO of the company, it's far easier to project negativity onto them, because their humanity allows it."

"I think I get what you're saying. So their strategy seems to be to provide an umbrella alternative to a human system that we all think is marred with error, and we'll choose it simply to avoid voting for a recognizable individual and their potential faults?"

"Yes. Frankly, it's fucking genius, and only the circle of people responsible for it know it. Bob's going to win. There's no way he can lose. When society as a whole would rather vote against someone than for someone, an entity like Bob provides the perfect blanket solution. Just like this invisible house right here. You can't destroy Robert Blytheswood's home. You can't knock off his mailbox with a baseball bat, or leave a pile of burning shit on his door, you can't protest out front of his house, or catch a candid audio clip while he's leaving for work in the morning. You can't fight him."

He pauses to light another smoke, and start the car back up.

"And you can't drive every single voter out to this vacant lot to explain why you can't fight him. Surely not on the eve of the election, of course. Alright, let's go."

"Keep it down in there!"

Keep it down? Fuck you. Fucking pig, Fuck. I've been trying to get your fucking attention for like an hour now. If these bars and sheets of plexiglass bullshit weren't here I'd make you my butt bitch right now. Why the fuck am I still in here?

When the fuck am I getting out?

"When the fuck am I getting out?"

"Getting out? You're not getting out. We're preparing to transfer you to County right now, just came to tell you to shut the fuck up. So, shut the fuck up."

Fuck you.

"Fuck you."

"Yeah? I'm not the one with a phone book of priors - on top of your current charges - and sitting in a jail cell right now, am I? I'm the least of your worries. Save your energy."

Wait. Did this fucking pig just say I'm getting transferred to County? Why the fuck would they be throwing me back in the bucket? What the fuck is he talking about?

"Wait. County? What the fuck you talking about? A night in the drunk tank isn't enough reason to hold me. Let me the fuck out of -"

"Settle down, buddy. We've got you fitting the description of a break and enter, as well as assault with a weapon. Hitting a sixty-eight year old man in his own home isn't too smart."

B&E? Assault? No. No-no-no-fuck-no-no-fuck. Fuck that. That piece of shit Santa fucker. He attacked me.

That piece of shit is lying.

"You mean that Santa fucker and his wizard friend? He attacked me! He's full of shit!"

"Right. He's 'full of shit'. You do realize that the old man you assaulted is not only a member of the town council, but actually plays Santa Claus in the Christmas parade? You - on the other hand - are a repeat offender. Prolific offender, even. I don't think you're going to convince anyone that Santa Claus is a liar. And if Santa did beat you up, it was probably because you were naughty."

I'll fucking 'naughty' the shit out of you right now. Fuckin'...

This is bullshit.

"This is bullshit! I fucki-"

"Yeah? Tell it to the judge, but for now just try to keep it down in here. You'll be shipped out within the hour."

Fuck you. I'll ship you out within the hour.
Bitch.

This should work, it has to work.
All this extra support should be just what it needed.
The fucking Zeppelin.
A modern marvel in engineering.
No.
Not really.

It's ugly as fuck.

Not properly engineered, nor artistically prepared.

Looks like a misshapen football.

Or a failed meatloaf recipe.

Who am I kidding. It looks like a bandaged up turd. A turd with a giant cardboard filter on one end so you could suck on the shit without it getting in your mouth.

It looks like shit.

But, it's smokeable shit. With all this weed, I couldn't stop myself from having a little bit of fun.

A sixteen paper joint. Four by four. Sweet sixteen.

Fuck yes.

Commence salivation.

I thought a quarter would do it, but I had to add an extra couple grams, fuck it. Why not?

Who's stopping me?

Oh, right. And the oil, of course.

Smeared thick like peanut butter. Smooth.

Made chunky with the weed.

That maybe wasn't the best idea.

That's what made it so heavy. Finally got the thing wrapped up but then it couldn't support it's own weight. All these extra Zig-Zag strips should help, though. Strengthen its cast.

So ugly, but that's what really gives it the Zeppelin look.

Along with the fact that I'm going to light it up like the Hindenburg. Fuck, I'm scared to even pick it up right now, in case it combusts and disintegrates right before my very eyes.

Would be a waste of engineering.

To break at the seams and fall to Earth so shortly after take off. Irony. I wonder if Droops is going to be back soon. He's not going to want to miss this one.

And I probably shouldn't smoke this beast alone.

Ah, the door's opening.

That's probably him there now.

His spidey sense was tingling, no doubt.

Unless it's Granger.

No, stop thinking that way.

He's gone.

Nope, it's Reef. Long time no see.

"Reef! How's it going? Ha, long time no see."

"Yeah, eh. Going good. Woah, shit. Place looks different. What the fuck?"

"Right?! Granger's gone!"

"He's gone? For real?"

"Fuck yeah. Like, 'gone gone'. Yesterday worked out quite well. I went out for a wander and the universe fixed itself."

"Nice. Ah, this is a buddy of mine I wanted you to meet."

"Ah, hey. Sorry, man. I'm Bob."

"Hey. Spudley."

"Spudley? Nice to meet you, man. Good timing. You guys want to smoke a joint?"

"Fuck, dude. Of course. Light it up. What you got going on here?"

"I call it, 'The Zeppelin'."

"Haha. That thing seriously looks like a piece of shit."

"Yeah well as long as it gets us fucked up it doesn't really need to win any contests, does it? Sixteen papers, like, ten grams of weed and almost two grams of oil are in this thing."

"And you were just rolling this for yourself?"

"Well, you guys, too. Been working on this for nearly an hour now, I figured someone would show up by the time I was done. I know she's not pretty, but she'll fly. Fuck it, I'm celebrating. Anyway yeah, dude. When I got home last night Granger had already been evicted. Landlord came and hauled his shit to the dump today, told me he's sitting in jail right now. So I've been redecorating, and reclaiming this space."

"Well fuck, eh. Looks good. And so, this weed?"

"Yup. Granger's."

"Figured. Well, fuck. That's a good turn of events. As long as it doesn't eventually come back around and bite you in the ass, eh? Plus, this really is a good pad."

"Definitely. And like I said, I'm celebrating. What you guys got going on tonight?"

"Not much, really."

"Well, let's drink. But for now, let's light up this Hindenburg. Been waiting an hour to say that."

"Mmmmhmhmh ffffmmmmfmffmfm mmmmm"

What the fuck is that?

"Mhhhmmmhmmmhmhmmmmmmmhmhmhmhmh"

Who the hell is that on the PA system down there?

Ah, fuck. It must be that Meat Draw bullshit going on downstairs. Seriously, can't a guy sleep until late afternoon in peace?

The hazards of living above a bar.

"Mhhhmffffmmmmmm hhhhhmmmmmm mmhmhhmh"

Yeah exactly.

Fuck, turn down the damn microphone. Seriously.

I have enough of a headache as it is.

Wonder what the kitchen special is today.

Monday? Club Sandwich?

Whatever it is, I should head down there soon.

I need some food.

Some meat.

"Mhhhhhmmmm mmmhhhhmhmhmhmh."

No, not from you 'Muffle Man'.

Turn down your fucking microphone.

There sure are a lot of ugly people in the world.

Seriously.

I mean, think about it. The average person really isn't very much to look at, and to paraphrase George Carlin: look at how homely the average person is, and then realize that half the world population is uglier than them.

That's a lot of ugly people, having ugly sex and making ugly offspring. Lumps of sweaty flesh rolling around dirty sheets in moldy bug-ridden homes across this land.

Gross.

So fucking gross.

Look at that dude.

Just look at his fucking face.

Fuck, I hope he didn't breed. Two chins, huge asymmetrical nose, pear-shaped body, and the haircut of a teenage army recruit. Probably has an IQ somewhere around his age. He's got that expression like he's still trying to remember where he left his last peanut butter cup, or if he actually ate it.

At least close your fucking mouth while you stare into space thinking about it.

I hate people whose faces rest with mouths open.

And what's with that weird old lady in all purple.

Her hair.

Oh, that must be a wig.

Too hideous to be real.

And over by the pool table, the only crowd in this place right now. Dumb, grizzled, trucker-types flanked by their tramp-stamped, bleach blonde, wrinkly MILF wannabes.

Pockets full of Meat Draw tickets, no doubt.

Disgusting.

Seriously.

Why?

Why are all these ugly people sitting around this dank bar at this hour?

Wait.

And why am I here?

Am I one of the ugly ones?

Nah. Not me. I just come to judge, and stare. Stare at these hideous people, loafing about.

I shouldn't gawk, But everyone is just so damn ugly in here.

Do ugly people gather here on purpose? Are they drawn to this place specifically?

I don't get it.

Maybe this place makes you ugly.

But seriously, attractive people don't drink here. I wonder where they go. This is the only bar like this in town.

Maybe it's a secret that only the few pretty people are privy to. Some other bar where spending an evening there is like being on a movie set, or an after party for a film premiere. Where bulbs aren't missing from the bathroom vanities.

Taken for sketchy purposes, no doubt.

There needs to be way more ugly people in bar scenes on TV. Shit's just not believable otherwise.

Fucking seriously.

But I guess you can't really put this sad batch of people on TV without viewers puking in their mouths a little. Retching at the reality of how ugly the common person is.

People disgust me.

Ewwww. Look at that guy. What's with the microphone?

"Alright, everybody! Time to pull out your tickets for the Meat Draw! Everyone got their tickets!"

Oh, fuck. That explains it.

Fuck this shit, I'm going for a smoke.

"Okay! First number is..."

Your microphone is too fucking loud, dude!

The smoke is so thick.

So. Thick.

I feel like I should care, but I couldn't possibly care about anything right now. Too baked. You could punch me in the face and I'd just go, "*Heeeeeeeeey*" like Ace Ventura being hit with a tranquilizer dart. Ten grams of weed is too much.

Oh yeah, the oil.

That's why it's burning so slow, and why the smoke is so thick. So. Thick. Damn. I'm baked.

Look at the smoke.

If there were batteries in the smoke alarm it would've gone off long ago. Definitely.

If the windows were open, the neighbours would see the smoke billowing out, and surely call 9-1-1.

Billow.

What a weird word. Like a pillow of smoke.

There's a mighty billow in here right now.

That's for sure.

It's comfortable against my head.

I feel like firefighters could hack down my door and barge in here at any moment.

Hahaha, and start a billow fight.

News reports eventually reveal it was some stoners blazing a Zeppelin.

Authorities are still on scene. Haha.
I'm so baked.

"Hey, does your TV work?"

"TV? Yeah, why?"

"I want to throw the news on, see what they're saying about the election."

"It's all a bunch of bullshit."

"Yeah, well I want to listen to it if I can."

Reef gets up, swims through the thick smoke over to the TV, and turns it on.

" - call this number now and order your copy of -"

" - but, Jenna, I love you. I thought that -"

" - after you add the onions, give the mixture time to -"

" - Praise Jesus. Say it with me, 'Praise -"

" - well, Bob, the next item up for bid is a -"

" - thank you Tom for that report, now let's turn to the election coverage with..."

He finds a generic news station then sits back down. I'm just tuning out the voices. Their grey, tired voices that would be just as suited for announcing golf games or curling matches as they are for politics. Same boring shit, different boring pile. It's not that I don't care about the election, but I just don't care what these losers have to say about it. Their paid opinions don't matter to me, especially when this Zeppelin is still floating around.

It just won't stop burning.

Besides, I can barely see the TV through the billow, anyway.

Hey, I recognize that mop.

"Fecma. How's it going?"

"Droopy McDroopnuts. How's it hanging?"

"Low and lazy, as usual. Fuck, I forgot about this Meat Draw bullshit."

"Yeah, man. Every Monday. And I can hear that stupid announcer guy right up through the floor into my suite. It's bullshit. Worse than karaoke night."

"Yeah, that microphone doesn't need to be that loud."

"Oh, fuck. Tell me about it. I think it's for all the old farts in there with hearing aids looking to score some cheap rib-eyes. Worried they're going to miss hearing their number over the sound of crunching peanuts echoing inside their empty heads. I fucking hate Mondays here."

"Come to think of it, that does explain all the ugly people."

"Huh?"

"Nothing, was just thinking to myself. Oh, so did you hear about Bob's roommate Granger? Dude got kicked out last night."

"Yeah, I know. I was the one who kicked him out."

"No, I mean - wait. Ha, he got kicked out of the pub last night, too? When did you start bouncing?"

"Yeah, well I figured might as well help out around here a bit. I mean, I'm here enough. Makes my rent cheaper upstairs, and I really do like roughing up drunks. Granger was a special treat. Covered my tab and everything. He won't be welcome back here ever again."

"Oh, I bet. Well, he's booted out of his basement suite now, too. Hey, what do you got going on tonight?"

"Fuck, eh. Hmmm, not much. They don't really need me around here on a Monday."

"Well, you should come out to Bob's tonight now that Granger's gone. We're planning on having some drinks and celebrating and shit."

"Fuck yeah. Sounds like a plan."

"Cool shit, well swing by whenever. I guess I'll see you later on. I was going to grab another beer but, well. Meat Draw people and all."

"No worries. Yeah, catch you later. Oh, hey. Do you know where I can score a sack? Not for me. The French guy upstairs. Lives a couple doors down from me. He's looking."

"French guy?"

"Yeah, I don't know. I think his name is Julian. Decent guy. Figured you might know where to score, seeing as how it looks like I can't go through Bob anymore."

"Actually, yeah. Granger's gone, but Bob should still have some. How much he looking for?"

"Just an eighth."

"Okay. Yeah, for sure. I'll head back to his place and send him up."

"Sweet, thanks."

"No worries, what room?"

"Fourteen."

"Fourteen. Cool. Maybe like, an hour?"

"Sounds good. I'll let him know."

"Yeah. Bob will probably just walk up here himself, or me. Okay, cheers. Fuck this Meat Draw bullshit, anyway. Just wanted to sit and have a quiet beer. Fuck."

"I hear ya. Cheers."

Well, that's cool. That'll earn Bob some extra drinking money for tonight. I should head back anyway, this place is depressing right now.

Meat Draw.

Whoever thought of raffling off packages of fucking meat in a bar is an idiot.

Seriously.

Winning the majority is key.

The Bob campaign won't work without totality.

There would have been no reason to put this much money, risk, and exposure into a plan that would've led to an opposition party easily suppressing any sort of imbalanced agenda.

They may have had chances in the past to pull off the ruse, but they couldn't risk any other party collectively holding more seats than Bob.

Any legal opposition would defy the entire plan.

How will the people react to this?

Even though they chose it?

The evidence and scrutiny will lie within the people.

They will either concede and accept what has happened, or denounce it as blasphemy and attempt to burn the witch at the stake. According to the statistics, they're too passive for witch burnings. They'll accept whatever happens.

As a majority, they'll agree to this.

This will be their choice.

What will be interesting to see though, is how all the people react who have lived their lives desperate for change. Those who have never had any input or opinion about what positive change might mean. All they know is that right now sucks, and hopefully the future will be brighter.

The future won't be brighter. It never is.

Especially when you view the world in generalities.

There will be bright days, there will be dark days.

Either way, they aren't any human's fault.

It must suck to be the person expected to fix something so broken.

I guess it's a good thing that no one knows who Bob is.

For now.

"Wait. What do you mean they're all 'Bobs'?"

"Well, like you for example. You're a 'Bob'. We aren't all collectively voting for one person named 'Bob' to run the country. Each riding is voting for an individual member to represent a seat within the House. Get it? But all these people, across the country are all named 'Bob' in some form or another. As far as I've figured out from my research, you could be one of the candidates. Except that you're a real person with a real address."

"Yeah I am. I've actually had a lot of fun thinking about this through the election. That voting for Bob is voting for me."

"Fuck yeah. Vote Bob. I'd vote for you, you're a solid dude. Actually, you want to have a party tonight, right? Why not an election party?"

"Yes. That. Exactly that. Let's do it."

"Make it so."

"Any excuse to have a party, right?"

"Works for me. Like I said, let's do it."

"Captain, the sensors are picking up an object at 742577 mark 3, approaching quickly."
"Put it on the main viewer."

The door opens and a figure breaches the smoke.

"Do what? And what's burning?"

"Ah, Droops. Fuck dude, you just missed out on an epic session."

"No worries. You want to make a sale?"

"Actually, no not really. Like, we literally just blazed most of Granger's weed, dude."

"Fuck, really? Reef? You know anyone?"

"Actually, Spudley here's got some -"

"Spudley? You're selling now and didn't tell me? Shame. What would your mother think?"

"Hey, this just kind of came up today. I tried to tell you about it this morning. And just because I still live at home doesn't mean I'm some sort of momma's boy."

"Sure, it doesn't."

"Fuck you."

"Whatever. Well, you want to make a sale or not? We just have to walk back up to the pub."

"Sure. How much?"

"An eighth?"

"Yeah, I've got that. Let's go."

"Well hey, I can give you guys a lift if you want?"

"Yeah, sweet. Thanks, Reef. Yeah let's do this. Alright. Bob, we'll be back in a bit."

"Sounds good. Oh, since you guys are heading uptown, want to grab me some booze for tonight?"

"Yeah, no worries. What did you want?"

"I don't know. Here's fifty bucks to chip in. Surprise me. Get as much booze as you can. We're going to try and pull an all-nighter."

"*Winning majority is key, and I think that's the goal here. They think they can achieve a majority on the backing of their current minority leadership, and so that's why they've called this early election. If you look back throu-*"

Fuck this news bullshit.

Now that everyone's gone, this drivel is getting shut off and replaced with music right quick.

This is my place.

I'm the only Bob that matters right now.

Let's see...what to throw on. Metal. Definitely metal.

Where's my CD booklet?
All my good shit.
Here we go.
Time for my music. My soundtrack. My score.
Something heavy.
Something dark.

Burzum.

Yes.

Ah, Varg. Haven't heard your voice in a while.
Go on. Contaminate the air.

I wonder how Granger is doing. Decked out in his orange jumpsuit, swearing at anything with a badge.

He's going to have a fun time in the bucket. Egotistical pieces of shit with no concept of respect usually do.

Nevermind that, though.
I have an appointment with Ea, Lord of the Depths...

"AAAAARRRRRGGGGHHHHHHH!!!"

"So. Spudley. You run upstairs and do your thing while Reef and I go grab the booze. We'll come back and grab you after."

"No worries. Catch you in a bit."

"Don't take too long."

"Trust me. I won't."

I always hate coming up here. Nothing against Fecma, but this place is sketchy. If there was ever a place in town that made me feel uncomfortable, it was here. Not the bar itself, the bar's fine. I've had many great nights at the Village Tavern, it's just -

Going upstairs is a whole different story.

Most people who drink in this building ignore the fact that these homes exist above them. These tiny cubicles that make up lonely people's lives. I think many of us feel like we're only a few steps in the wrong direction away from being one of these people.

I find it hard to think that I could someday be one of these people. I'm younger than nearly everyone who frequents here.

Except Fecma.

Fecma's lived here for years now.

Somehow, he rented a room up in this rat cage when he was sixteen and has never left. I don't know how he does it. He's tough, but he can't be that tough. And he's far too young to possibly fit in with the age and history of this place.

The building is ancient compared to our lifetimes.

From what I've heard through drunken bar stories, it had its best years during the prohibition era. I don't think the decor has changed much since then, so their stories are easy to picture in your head through the grizzled slurs.

For the regulars who've spent their evenings for the last forty years - drinking themselves away beneath the dim lighting - they possibly preferred the familiar setting and the memories this building holds, but for the people who lived above it I always considered it one of the worst places - and ways - to live in this town. Don't ask me why. It's just a feeling I get from this place.

My own opinion.

Some may say it's haunted.

I say it's just piles of dirty laundry.

Unclean and unsorted thoughts, left to pile and rot.

This place could use a garbage chute.

Or a few.

Metaphorically speaking. Fuck.

The stairs themselves are a drunkard's nightmare. Wide and

narrow, without railings on either side and abnormally long in order to accommodate the vaulted ceiling below.

A place for thoughts to float like a cloud line if you will, shrouding the peak above.

Fuck, that Zeppelin joint thingy really messed me up.

Maybe it's the thin air up here, too.

At the summit, the hallway extends to the left and right, before turning corners down long corridors that hold the numbered human cages. So clinical. So depressing.

I hate this place.

I hate this place so much.

Every door frame bears the history of repeated kick-ins. Surgery scars of locks removed and replaced, wood scrap patchwork, dents, holes, peeled paint, and one hundred years of gravity wearing away the form of the structure itself.

This place could crumble to the ground at any moment.

Sometimes a sale isn't worth it.

Sometimes a person is not worth meeting.

Fuck.

I don't know how any person could possibly win the battle within themselves - or lose, I suppose - to accept willingly living here. I can't help but wonder how many people have died in their sleep behind these doors - or are currently sleeping, dead - simply waiting for the smell to arouse suspicion.

This is where minds go to give up and die.

No, I'm being blindly judgmental.

Stop it.

Almost at this French dude's room.

Number 14.

Fuck, what was his name?

I guess it doesn't really matter. He thinks my name is Bob. Well, he thinks that's my name because Fecma told him that's who'd be coming. Works for me, though. I mean, I'm sure Bob won't mind if I just go with it. Besides, I don't even think that's Bob's real name, either.

He doesn't look like a 'Bob' - and I really don't want to meet new people. Not here to make a friend.

Not here.

A knock upon a damaged door.

A moment and it opens.

"Allo Bohb? Eese deese Bohb?"
"Hey, man. How's it going?"
"Goud. Eeet eese goud. Nice to meet you. 'Ow are you?"
"I'm good, man. I'm good."
"Goud. Come een."
"Thanks."

Inside. Out of the creepy hall.

Although inside the rooms was barely safer than being in the hall, it gives me some comfort going in and hearing the bolt lock behind us.

Jail cells are more comforting than these quarters.

The only selling point is a window that opens, but I suppose if that's the only thing you have it doesn't really give much comfort. Not much of a luxury. A sanctioned necessity.

A place from which to jump.

You couldn't kill yourself from this height, though.

I'm sure that's a common conclusion here.

Unfortunately.

An old, rusty sink with exposed pipes grows out from the rust on the far wall, and the only other feature of the room is the bed - more of a cot, really - and a tiny table with a single chair.

No need for two. No space for two.

Visitors to this place are rare, and if it happens, the host will take the bed as a seat. Offering up the relatively clean chair.

Like what is happening now.

He motions. I sit. He sits.

I hate being here, but at least I don't live here.

How do you do it, Fecma?

I'll live at home forever rather than subject myself to this voluntary imprisonment. Sorry, but fuck this.

At least I'm not forced to hate it here.
I don't have to live with the hate.
I just might have to visit it now and then.
In order to make a shady sale.

I'm a drug dealer now.

I don't know.
I always think of weed as not even being a drug.
I mean, it's a plant. Unaltered. Smoked. Done casually.
But, watching him eye up the bag,
pull out a choice nugget,
begin cutting it up meticulously with gummed up scissors onto a department store flyer,
reach for the last of his papers,
peck one out of the pack -
Go through this ceremony, of sorts.

Just so he can roll a joint.

Watching him, I can't help but see the drug. I can't help but see the fiend behind it. I think that's why I hate coming here. I hate seeing weed living here, alongside other drugs. I don't think it belongs here.

This is something I'm probably going to have to get used to.

"Stay to smoke?"

No. Just go.

"Sure, man."

I'm definitely going to have to work on being less polite, too.

"According to the latest polls, the -"

"Do you mind putting on some music or something, Reef? Seriously. Fuck this election shit. It's all bullshit."

"My car. I want to hear it."

"Fine. You do know that it's not going to change anything though. Right?"

"What won't?"

"This election."

"Of course things will change. How long has anything really gone without changing? Things always change."

"Sharks."

"Sharks?"

"Sharks don't change."

"Yeah, but sharks don't need to change."

"Exactly. Nothing changes in our system because it's run by sharks. Ancient sharks with no need to change."

"You mean that the system is run by dinosaurs."

"No, I mean fucking sharks. Dinosaurs are dead. Sharks watched them die. From the water and shit."

"Yeah but, you can't fuck with a shark. It's different."

"Exactly. And because you can't fuck with a shark, nothing changes. Something needs to fuck with a shark, I guess."

"Ha. Did you just say you want to fuck a shark?"

"No. Fuck *with* a shark. With."

"You want to fuck with a shark?"

"No. Fuck. Fuckin'. Sharks. They need to get fucked with. Someone needs to fuck with them. Not me. I don't fuck sharks."

"Sure you don't. Whatever, shark fucker."

"Shut up. I was just trying to prove a point. What's taking Spudley so long?"

"I don't know, but fuck this. I'm sick of waiting. He can walk back to Bob's from here."

"Yeah, it's not that far. Let's just head back with the booze."

"What did you end up getting, anyway?"

"It's a surprise. Let's go."

...surprises aren't always good.

"Malt liquor? Seriously?"
"You said to surprise you."
"Yeah, but -"
"Surprise!"
"What the fuck? Reef, why'd you le-"
"Woah, I had nothing to do with this. I just drove him th-"
"You said to get as much booze as I could. This was the most cost effective way."

Fuck.

Seventeen.

Seventeen forty ounce bottles of Olde English.
This is a terrible idea.

"But, malt liquor? Really? That was a stupid idea."
"I don't know, felt like switching it up. Plus, it's cheap. We needed enough booze to stay up all night, right? No way we're drinking all of this."
"No way we're staying up all night off of this sloppy shit, either."
"Booze is booze."
"Nah, man. This is malt liquor. Fuck. I don't know about tonight."
"Just stop fucking complaining. Fine, here. Take your money back. The booze is on me, 'Bob's Pre-Election Party' or whatever

the fuck you want to call it, okay? You should've been more specific if you were going to get picky after the fact. Fuck."

Well, since he's paying I'll shut the fuck up.

I grabbed one, took a swig, grimaced, and took another hoping it would taste better.

Now I'm just staring at him again.

But he's right. I am picky.

I shouldn't have asked to be surprised.

I'm surprised.

Another swig. Another grimace.

It's like dipping your foot in cold water and then dipping it again hoping you've already adjusted.

Nope. Fuck.

This is going to be a brutal night.

After this bottle I'm definitely going to the beer store on my own.

I can't drink this shit 'til morning.

"Spudley! How goes?"

"Ah, hey man. Figures I'd run into you."

"Yeah. I saw you from the window, figured I'd come down."

"Cool shit. I'm waiting for Reef and Droops to get back, but I'm kinda thinking they ditched me."

"Yeah, sounds like a Droops thing to do. I saw him earlier. But Reef, eh? He's out and about? How's he doing?"

"Better, but - you know."

"Yeah. I get it. So, you heading over to Bob's?"

"That's the plan. Just needed to drop off some weed to a French guy here but got stuck smoking one."

"Ah, Julian? Yeah, he'll do that. Good guy, though."

"I guess. But, now I'm out of a fuckin' ride."

"Well, fuck it. I'm planning on heading there, too. It isn't far, but I'm lazy. I'll get us a cab. How about we go into the bar. I'll have them phone one for us. We'll have a couple beers while we wait."

"Sounds like a plan."

"So, wait. You delivered to Julian? Granger's weed, or you selling now?"

"Selling. Yeah, I actually came into some good fortune. I'll explain inside."

"So, we're going to stay up all night drinking, and then go vote when the polls are open?"

"Yup. That's the plan."

"What's the fucking point?"

"In drinking or voting?"

Droops stopped and thought it, and a look grew on Bob's face like he was watching an animal sniff around a baited trap. He changed the subject and avoided commenting on the question, but it lingered in my mind.

What was the point in drinking all night?
What was the point of voting?
But that's just relativity.

You can overthink anything into absurdity.

In reality there is no point in anything, really. Existence itself is futile by nature. I guess the point of drinking is to ignore the heavy cloud of futility that hangs over life. A controlled distraction in a distracting, chaotic world.

The point is to not dwell on any sort of point.

So why vote?

Why spend all night ignoring and shaming the system in preparation for a small moment of its acknowledgment?

Maybe it takes hours of focused ignorance to spend a short moment allowing awareness?

Awareness of the futility?

I'm already getting a buzz.

And probably thinking more about this than I should.

I can't seem to get this election stuff off of my mind, though.

The door's opening. Someone's here.

Ah, Spudley and Fecma.

Feels good, hanging out with everyone again.

"Fecma! How's it going?"

"Reef! Goes good. Heard you were here. Good to see you. Ah, so Bob. I've got a story for you. Ran into your roomie at the bar last night..."

They start talking, as do Droops and Spudley, and I slowly get lost in thought again.

What will it mean if Bob wins this election?

Because the more I think about it, the more he looks positioned to take the win easily. There's usually fear attached to the unknown, but at the moment I'm just confused.

What I do know is that I've never seen such meticulous thought and planning put into a political campaign ever. Intricacy hiding behind simplicity. It seems basic and cryptic on the surface, but it takes an extensive amount of skill to achieve such simplicity. Especially within a complex system that withstands a constant scrutiny of its methods.

How is something able to remain so cryptic while still being accepted by the...

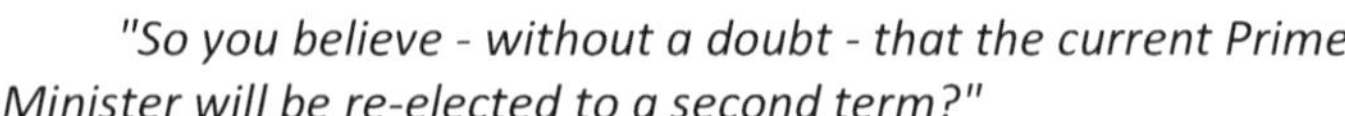

"So you believe - without a doubt - that the current Prime Minister will be re-elected to a second term?"

"Most definitely."

"Yet early polls and statistics seem to show that the leading party is trailing the opposition at the moment, significantly."

"Possibly. But I don't think those numbers are entirely accurate. You have to remember that these sort of surveys are limited in their scope, and that these types of 'foresight' have been proven to be highly inaccurate."

"That may be true, but it still doesn't explain how you can be so certain that the Prime Minister is going to achieve re-election."

"Well, I think the party itself feels rather certain about their re-election. If you look at the real numbers - such as the current Prime Minister's approval ratings and his work to cut the deficit - the basis for predicting a re-election seems logical. Look at the approval rating alone. Although he's currently sitting at forty-one percent - which may not seem considerably high - it's important to note that he has consistently hovered around that percentage throughout his term. I don't feel that the people of this country will be so quick as to remove him from office without having considerable disdain for him. He's still respected by the people. He's done nothing wrong, and I don't feel that we have any need to go and switch horses at the moment."

"But some would argue, just because he may not have done anything wrong it doesn't mean he's done anything right either. Besides his questionable tactics to decrease the national deficit, what other major policy advancements have happened during his time in office thus far? What major contributions have really been provided to our society during this first term? I think what you're trying to say is that he has been playing it safe the past four years, and I don't believe that's what the people of this country want to

see in their leader. Sometimes risks need to be taken. By a leader, and by its people."

"But you forget that he still struggles with a minority government, which limits the ability to affect policies to any significant extent."

"So then, you believe they hope to achieve a majority government this time around."

"Everyone hopes to achieve a majority government, both on the sides of the elected party and the people who elect them. It's the only way to truly make advancements within the rigid political system. So yes, of course that's what I believe."

"And how likely is that?"

"That actually is a complicated question. It's a conversation that all of us analysts have been having around the water cooler. The honest answer is, we really don't know."

"And why is that?"

"Well, you're going to make me say it aren't you? It's because of the 'Vote Bob' campaign. It's just too hard to predict. There's no precedent, and very little information available. No one I've talked to has really seen anything quite like it in their years spent covering elections, or can find much reference to anything like it before our time. So, everyone is hesitant to give them any credibility, or to really take any stance at all. It's a tough one. What I will say though, is that it has made for an interesting campaign and we're all excited to see the results tomorrow."

"As are we. Thank you again for your time. I'm sure you're extremely busy today, being the eve of the election."

"Definitely, it's been a wild day here."

"I'm sure it has. Okay. Now, we will take you live, to the election headquarters of the current opposition party, where we have Samantha standing by..."

More pundits spewing bullshit.

Pay for the cab and head into Bob's to relax.

A forty gets thrust into my face.

Half of it's gone before I realize it.

It's surprising that I've never met Bob before now, considering the cross-section of people I do know who are all here at his place. I don't know what to make of him, really. Not yet at least. I've never met anyone quite like him before.

He's damaged, obviously - just like the rest of us - but he wears his damage well. Most people hide their damage.

Their scars. I do.

It's almost like...well...

It's not like he's showing them off, it's more like they're just there. His scars are in plain sight, and there's no effort made to cover them up.

And his guard is down.

Ah, his guard is down.

There are no defensive tactics on display.

That's what it is.

He's making no effort to protect himself.

Odd.

What if he gets attacked?

He's obviously been attacked before. Wouldn't that make you want to defend yourself more fully?

I guess that wouldn't happen amongst this chosen crowd.

Maybe he has a hidden strength I can't see.

Or, maybe he's just actually comfortable with who he is.

I can't find much fault in that perspective.

Obviously this is his place, this is his home. If we were somewhere else I'm sure it would be different, but he's almost radiating a comfort - like, 'you can't hurt me here and no one else is likely to be hurt while here, so leave your weapons at the door.' - and everyone is actually genuinely relaxed.

That's rare when you gather any amount of people into a

small space and feed them booze. This many egos.

Egos.

That's what it is.

Not weapons, egos.

I don't know how he did it, but it's almost like everyone left their weathered ego at the door upon entering, like a pair of shoes or an umbrella. There's a pile of something that he made us all leave beside the door, and we can retrieve it when we go.

Returned. To be put back on.

Interesting.

I'm not used to partying like this. There's always at least one idiot getting progressively drunker and louder to the point where you need to keep a constant eye on him.

At least one. Usually many.

In comparison, you can't even really call this a party.

What do you call a half dozen people sitting in a room getting drunk and talking over background music about politics and whatnot?

Sounds like the lead up to a bad joke.

A bad joke with no punchline.

Vote Bob.

"Everything gonna be alright.
Everything gonna be alright. Yeah."

Bottles everywhere.

This place gets messy quick.

I don't mind, though. This is a fun mess.

It's my mess.

This is my place.

That's still going to take a while to sink in.

"I went deep down into that river. Now I rose up.
And I felt that sun beat down upon this sinner's face. Yeah."

I wanted to go to the beer store.

I wanted something other than this piss.
I hate malt liquor.

But now I'm getting buzzed.
And I don't care as much anymore.

Fuck it.

"I climbed the highest of heights.
Atop that mountain I watched the day turn into night."

Booze is booze.
Take what's offered.
Don't be a bitch.
It's all good.
I'll survive.

"Rubbing needles in my eyes. Eating dirt.
I stood up and everything was alright."

The booze has definitely kicked in. Someone mentioned the election and now we all have the perspectives of political analysts.
Reef convinced the room to put the news back on.
Bad idea.

We're not people anymore.
We're a room of drunken opinions.

"But that's exactly what I mean. We all have this fallacy that our voice is meaningless, and our individual 'X' means nothing because we are a generation of individuals. A generation of lonely ideologists who don't think anyone else could possibly think the way we do, so any attempt at organizing into a collective is futile based on this isolated nature of the individualistic necessity.

"A society of snowflakes, but together we can whip up one hell of a storm. We never stop to realize that we outnumber baby-boomers. Maybe sometimes we do, but we quickly brush off that fact - or its importance - because we assume that even though we have superior numbers we have a much broader range of belief systems. This false assumption leads us to believe that we could never possibly agree upon any one thing - even remotely – the way the boomers were able to seemingly organize in their time.

"We give up without trying, and that's exactly what was hoped of us. Scatter us so thinly, and sub-categorize us so extensively that we couldn't ever possibly think that beyond our flamboyant individuality lies similar feelings and morals.

"They made us fight ourselves, and we're doing it, even here amongst similar minds who exist within similar variables we're arguing the merit of thinking alike. I find it strange that it is difficult for us to trust someone who we understand as being a similar mind, one that also finds it difficult to trust others. The acceptance of this futility has allowed the things we detest to maintain their momentum and grow like a snowball - rolling down a hill - while we sit and argue the pointlessness of ever trying to catch up to it."

"So you're saying that punks and hippies and metal-heads and crackheads and ravers and skaters all need to unite and overtake the machine?"

"I think I'm saying that we're already far more united than we realize. If we only saw how close we already were to believing in the same thing - and wanting the same change - then we wouldn't waste so much effort avoiding unification. We'd quickly move beyond that stubbornness to a point where we start understanding each other and seeing ways that we have always been unified without knowing it."

"Ha, and that's the point?"

"It's 'a' point. I don't think there's a single holy place where we can all converge and find the answer all at once. I think it's fleeting, and exists across a multitude of spectrums. Right place, right time, right perspective, and then an aspect of unification will reveal itself. Capture it, control it, and move on to the next one."

"Like Pokémon, gotta catch 'em all."

"Well, maybe more like a puzzle, but you need enough pieces before you can begin assembling it."

"And we have all these different people holding on to their pieces of the puzzle, not willing to add them to the pile."

"Exactly. Of course the puzzle seems impossible when you know you're missing pieces."

"Ha, yeah. Like a maze with no ending."

"Or a car with no wheels."

"This makes me think of that whole 'we only use fifteen percent of our brain' thing. What was the voter turnout last election? I don't really pay attention to numbers and stats and shit, but it was well under fifty percent. Right?"

"Thirty-six point four percent. They just showed it on the news."

"There you go. Imagine if you could somehow increase that percentage. If you could double the amount of voter power. You would be waking up all these dormant individuals, and if you could wake up that many, what would they do?"

"I understand what you're saying, but you're using a weird way of saying it. The one hundred percent brain function thing is sort of taken out of context. Picture it like using one hundred percent of a car. That would mean your headlights, high-beams, heater, air conditioning, radio, wipers, turn signals, hazards, gas, brakes, everything - all that shit - were all functioning simultaneously. There's a lot of opposites and contrasts to consider. Things that need to be 'off' so that others can be 'on' and functioning efficiently."

"Like ones and zeros."

"Exactly. Ones and zeros. Fifty percent would be maximum output, because every zero would subtract from it. Every switch can't just be on. Everything can't be doing everything all at once. But, with the voter thing, that's completely different. If you were to double the voters, and wake up that many dormant voters - oh, for sure - it would make a dramatic impact on the outcome of the election. On the simplest level, let's say you stand on a street corner taking a survey asking people what their favorite colour was, right? So you stand there all day asking people if they want to take a survey, and at the end of the day maybe one hundred people agree to your survey and you use those one hundred people to create a cross-section of what the population's favorite colours are.

"Well, the entire survey is bullshit. You know nothing about what everyone's favorite colour is, you only know the most common favourite colours amongst people who are willing to take surveys. Every single person who refused to take your survey still has a favourite colour, and their opinions or preferences never get calculated. What if in reality - out of the eighty five percent of people who chose not to do the survey, or whatever - sixty percent of them chose the same favorite colour? well then whatever colour most chosen by the fifteen percent of people surveyed - no matter what the percentage - would fall second compared to that of the unsurveyed. It's a bullshit system."

"No one's ever asked me to take a survey."

"There you go. There's that, too. The unasked, but willing to comply. What sort of percentage does that make up? You can't possibly ask everyone."

Now that I think of it, I have only ever taken a survey once. It was after getting home from high school one day, sitting watching cartoons, eating Oreo cookies and cheese slices - burnout munchies from an extensive lunch hour session chosen over eating - I picked up the phone while still sprawled lazily across the couch and the overly polite voice on the other end asked me if I had time to answer a few questions.

Of course I did, I had all the time in the world, and the show currently on didn't interest me at all.

He proceeded to ask me what brands of beverages I preferred, and what products I was familiar with, asked me about various things I may be considering buying in the upcoming months, and I answered everything truthfully. As truthfully as a fifteen year old kid would.

The questions went on for some time - I have no idea how long because at no moment did I feel the need to disengage the quizzical conversation and check the time - and I just kept answering questions as quickly as he could ask them.

Finally, it reached a point where he thanked me for my answers, and I acknowledged him indifferently. It was no skin off my back. It actually killed some time in which my brain wouldn't have done much of anything otherwise. The survey was over.

He thanked me, and then asked permission before getting personal information.

Whatever.

Name, gender, ethnicity, other things.

That's when things changed. I remember him saying,

'And how old are you, sir?'

It was one of the first times I had been called 'sir', and it felt awkward. To be honest, it still kind of does.

'Fifteen.'

I said honestly, and I felt the conversation shift.

'Oh.'

I remember hearing.

'Well, is your father home by chance?'

'Nope, just me. My Dad will be home soon.'

'Okay then, sorry to bother you. I'll try back another time.'

I wasn't bothered. Just confused as to why my answers

suddenly didn't matter.

Weird thoughts.

I need another beer.

Oh man, I'm getting pretty drunk.

My brain is swimming.

It feels good, though. A refreshing dip.

Cooling my temperature.

Part of me keeps wanting to think about things.

Dissect thoughts like cadavers.

Slap down the bag of onions that are ideas and keep peeling back the layers. Just keep peeling and dissecting - digging deeper - and seeing who cries first.

One of Me and Myself's favourite past times.

But we both know,

that's quickly becoming impossible.

The bag is rotten, infested. Full of bugs and an acrid stench disrespectful to expose in public.

Impolite.

More so, not necessary.

The rotten produce should be discarded. There's nothing more of value to be learned from its contents.

Besides, there is no table, no flat surface. No knife to cut the onions.

No target.

So even if I wanted to, I couldn't.

Everything is "fuck it" right now.

Alcohol makes the clothes fall off.

Physically, and mentally.

Assuming you have a mind.

Which I know everyone here does.

One of the reasons I like these guys.

Fuck.

I missed these dudes.

Why was I wallowing in sadness for so long?

Swimming around in my own bag of rotting onions with knives for arms.

Stupid.

This makes so much more sense to me. To my health. To my mental well-being. This is like taking a dip in a hot spring after sitting in used bathwater for days. Weeks, even.

Here, we're all skinny-dipping.

There's no armour being worn here.

Anyone can take their clothes off, it's a bit more of a challenge to achieve the same thing with the mind.

Taking the mind's garments off, and leaving them at the door like an overcoat. Or a hat, mask, or set of fairy wings. A piece of costume out of context, hung up to rest from the elements while they drain from the fabric.

Those elements puddle upon the floor and then dissipate without notice.

The hands of the clock wave a couple times, but nobody notices.

"Dude, Fecma's passed out!"

"We should shave his head! Bob, do you have clippers?"

"Yeah, actually. I think so."

Wait? What? Woah.

That escalated quickly.

I don't know who thought this was a good idea.

And, Bob. Seriously?

He doesn't seem like the type of guy to readily supply clippers to Droops so he can play Brutus the Barber Beefcake on his unsuspecting victim. Such a bad idea.

The vibe here has shifted drastically.

Common sense is deteriorating.

This was supposed to be a safe place.

It's the malt liquor's fault at this point, really.

It's given us new egos

that have found the weapons

hiding within tools.

In this case clippers.

Now that Fecma is sitting up - rubbing his eyes - everything that has led up to this moment keeps looping through my mind and I can't believe we kept going with it.

I can't believe he didn't wake up.

Between the mechanical buzz of Bob's trimmers and five drunkards hysterically laughing with every swipe across his skull it's truly amazing it got this far.

Fecma is still struggling to regain his vision with only a Krishna style ponytail of hair left hanging off of the corner of his head.

It was the only bit of his blonde locks that remained. They only managed to survive the harvest by hiding between his skull and the pillow it rested on.

He keeps rubbing at his eyes.

I just realized that he hasn't noticed the hair yet.

Oh, fuck. Here it comes.

His hands are traveling upwards towards his hairline.

Fingers begin pushing shaving cream around his face.

What the fuck were we thinking?

This was a terrible fucking idea.

Someone should have stopped this, but we couldn't.

We were all laughing too hard.

Why?

Fecma's going to kill us. All of us. He's easily the toughest person in this room. Why did we poke the bear - with clippers - repeatedly across his skull?

Stupid, stupid, stupid.

And why are we still here watching the bear wake up?

Rising from hibernation.

Pushing shaving cream into his own eyes.

We need to leave.

We need to leave right now.

He's going to start hurting the first person he sees.

How the hell could we have been that dumb?

We just fucking shaved Fecma's head.

What the fuck were we thinking?

"What the -"

Yup. We should go. We should go now.

"What the fuck?! What happened to my hair?!"

"You've been drafted, soldier!"

Bob? No, don't add more fuel to the fire you fucking idiot.

Just shut up, walk away.

I wasn't expecting this.

What the fuck is Bob doing? From who he was before, this seems completely out of character.

Now he's saluting Fecma. Stone-faced.

I'll admit, it's ballsy. But not funny.

Not a time to be amused, not at all.

This guy is going to kill us once he starts wiping shaving cream out of his eyes rather than into them. Then we're all fucked.

"What the fuck?! What the fuck?! Who shaved my fucking head?!"

"Step in line, soldier!"

Fecma grasps randomly at objects on the table, finds something of decent weight, and blindly chucks it towards Bob's voice. It ricochets off the wall a foot wide.

Yeah, we need to go.

This Bob guy's just laughing now. Laughing hysterically with his hand still across his forehead in full salute and a forty ouncer in the other, while Fecma stumbles over the table trying to close in on his location.

What a strange character.

"Your aim is pathetic, soldier!"

"What the fuck did you do to my hair?!"

"Silence, maggot! We donated it. To make wigs for cancer patients. You did a good thing! You should be proud, soldier!"

Bob just keeps fucking with him. Doesn't he know he's going to get hit?

And then he does.

Wham.

Mid-laughter.

Fecma closes the gap, swings his head, and connects firmly across Bob's jaw. A streak of blood within a firework of shaving cream splashes outwards from the collision.

I thought I had Bob somewhat figured out, but now I'm confused all over again.

We were gone before the entire scene could settle.

"So now what?"

"We give them some time, and then we go back."

And that's exactly what we did.

This feels old school.

Lined up along the wall of a closed convenience store sipping forty ouncers. Chiilin'. Like villains. Old school.

Ghetto, more like it.

The streets are dead silent. We sit there slowly swiggin' – our breaths steaming lightly in the air - as a single sound begins to form in the distance.

A repetitive squeak, with a dynamic rhythm.

Slowly getting louder. Closer.

What the fuck is that sound?

Squuuueak, squueeeeak, squeeeeaaaak.
Squueeeeak, squuuuueeeeak, squuueeeeaaaak.

It's coming this way.

Squueeeeaaaaak, squueeeeeeeak, squeeeeeeaaak.

A migrant worker on a bicycle wheels into sight, rolls down the sidewalk, veers into the parking lot of the convenience store, and then continues to spiral inwards like a snail shell.

Circling, circling, circling tighter until

he collapses

and falls asleep

at its center.

Yup, he's out cold.

"Ummmm. Did that just happen?"

"Yup. I think so."

"That dude's still laying there, so yeah. That definitely just fucking happened."

"Well, should we do something about it?"

"Nah, he'll be fine. Just needs to sleep it off."

"Yeah, but - I don't really want to sit here staring at him."

"He definitely killed the vibe."

"Think it's safe to go back yet?"
"Not yet."
"Damn. I guess maybe we should wander a bit?"
"Yeah. Let's go."

By this point we could hear him snoring.
His hoarse rumble faded behind us as we picked up the pace.

"Then I got my wings and I never even knew it.
When I was a worm, thought I couldn't get through it."

"Fuck, that hurt. I deserved that. You feel better, Fecma?"

"No, I don't. What the fuck, dude? You fuckin' shaved my head. Why the fuck would you shave my head?"

"Why would you headbutt a person? Just punch me like a normal fucker! Who headbutts? Honestly?"

"I like to headbutt. It's reflex."

"Ha. Well, now that I can see your skull, I understand why."

"Just shut the fuck up, dude."

"I know. Sorry."

"Fuck! I just want to knock you out all over again but it won't do any good now. Where'd everyone else go?"

"I think they fucked off for a bit until things calm down around here."

"Things as in me?"

"Ha, yeah. Obviously."

"Well, what's done is done. Things are calm."

"Are they?"

"Yeah."

"Yeah, but they don't know that. For all they know you're tearing me and my apartment to bits right now. Fuck that hurt.

How long was I out for?"

"Only a couple minutes. I went and washed off the fucking shaving cream - finished up where you guys fucking missed - and I could already hear you starting to mumble when I got back."

"Well, that's not bad then."

"I guess so. Got all your teeth?"

"Got 'em all still. Just cut my lip real good."

"Good."

"Yup, fair enough. Well, cheers. And truce?"

"Truce. Cheers. Going to be fun explaining this to the drunks at the bar. Fuck"

"Nah, you look good. *You look fuckin' scary*."

"Just shut up."

"Sorry. I'm done."

"Oh, by the way. You want to try one of these pills? It might make this groggy ditch water go down a bit better. My buddy Dave's got a bunch of these things."

"What are they?"

"They'll fuck you up pretty good."

"Yeah, but what are they?"

"Do you want one or not?"

"I'm just not sure if I trust you right now."

"Nah, it's fine. One won't do much anyway."

"Sure, fuck it. Hand one over."

"It'll keep you awake. You need to stay awake."

"Do I? Why's that?"

"It's for your own safety. You could have a concussion. Actually, I'd be surprised if you didn't. Plus, we still need to vote."

"Right. Voting. That was the whole point of this, right?"

"Yeah, it was. You definitely have a concussion."

"Because today is black.
Because there is no turning back."

"You sure these things'll keep me awake?"

"Oh, it'll keep you awake. But here, only do one."

"Where'd you get these from?"

"Don't worry about it. Just eat it."

I'm mildly worried.

I don't tend to trust Droops with anything, let alone random pills being handed out in the darkness of a quiet side street.

But I ate it.

Wish that store was open, now we're stuck walking to the next closest one. Some food might help me get through this night. I'm glad Reef suggested going for munchies, though.

I like having a plan.

Droops runs ahead and kicks over a lonely newspaper box.

It echoes down the empty, silent street.

Why are we doing this again?

Why are we wandering the streets in search of salty snacks?

Right. Vote Bob.

There's two of the signs right there in front of me.

But, yeah. Food.

Food is important.

Droops walks back over, triumphant. What a fucking idiot.

"We should go get some real food while we're out. Fuck snacks."

"Yeah, most places are closed and I ain't walking all the way out to Tim Horton's."

"That pizza place up the road?"

"Only delivery at this hour. They lock the door to keep people like us from fucking with them at night."

"Makes sense."

"What's wrong with that little East Indian gas station? They've got chips and shit."

"Pepperoni sticks. I just want pepperoni sticks."

"But that's not real food. Fuck it. Yeah. Let's just do that. By the time we get back things should've settled down at Bob's."

"Yeah. That was the plan."

"Fuck. Just shut up with the fucking plans already. 'That was the plan'. Fuck. Give me a smoke."

We continued our stroll down the sidewalk, with no clue how much we were stumbling at this point.

I don't fucking care.

All I want are some pepperoni sticks.

"So cold in space.
Infinitely stretching. Filled but empty."

Alcohol is referred to as a depressant, and I don't think that's quite accurate. I mean, I tend to drink to avoid depression. Same reason I smoke pot, or pop random pills.

To escape.

To simply avoid the world around us for a while. That's where most of the depression stems from. Our environment. I don't think it's within us, it's around us. Applying pressure.

It's a hard thing to ignore, but the booze helps to completely forget about how fucked up the world outside really is, or the imbalance of equity. I could live comfortably for a year with the money it costs for a celebrity's handbag, while millions can't afford food. Money has really fucked things up.

But, whatever. Not worth the wasted thought.

The mind never sleeps. It never stops thinking. It feels good to give it a break now and then and live in the moment rather than worrying about all the trivial details regarding everyday life.

To be able to just say 'fuck it all' now and then.

Yeah. Fuck it.

The mind is constantly forced to think, and it over-exerts itself with meaningless hypothetical scenarios that just lead to stress. Too much stress. The 'what ifs' can kill you. Fuck 'em all.

These timeouts are therapy.

"The sound, the hum.
The vibration of the nameless one.
While on Earth we create misery.
Cannot hear the wordless chanting."

Fuck, I'm drunk. Swimming.

Head bobbing up and down with the waves.

I don't know what it is about malt liquor, though. It's such a sloppy drunk. So fucking sloppy.

I mean - I'm drunk, but - I don't know if I like this kind of drunk. The room is swimming, but I'm just not feeling it.

I don't feel like swimming.

Fun. No. Not fun.

A whole night of this, eh?

What time is it? The clock is shivering.

Almost three? Is that right? Almost three. Three.

Three? Three what?

I thought this was a party. Some party.

Down to just me and Fecma.

Yay.

Not even worth blowing up balloons anymore.

Not like I was going to anyway.

The other guys probably all went home and are fast asleep by now. Full of cake and ice cream.

Fuckers.

"As I listen to the bliss I hear the hum of the universe,
I don't know what the truth is to this life."

"Well, this is boring."

"They'll be back soon. Probably went for munchies."

"Who will?"

"Reef, maybe. Spudley even, but not Droops. Droops - at the very least - will be back. Feeling those pills yet?"

"Pills? I don't know, maybe a little."

"How's your head? You doing okay?"

"I don't know, maybe a little."

"Haha, alright. Well, I need to switch this music to something with a bit more energy. Fuck this depressing, droney, depressing shit. It's not meshing with my buzz."

"Go for it, put on whatever you want. I need to take a piss."

"Don't fall in."

Three in the morning pretends that it is awake, with its lights shining in places where people never sleep.

But it's not.

Shadows passing through vulnerable chasms, scurrying to the next sheltered canopy while the flick of my lighter attempts to break the night's concentration.

Sounds echo farther than they would at other hours. Shifting points of origin as they bounce from slumbered walls and tired concrete. Uninhibited.

There's an eerie sense of peace in the air right now.

The law sleeps silently behind schoolhouses while the sound of bending metal soars up into the sky from somewhere.

It's a curiosity, observing what is awake while the majority sleeps.

There's a bird circling,

chirping,

and mocking my concept of freedom.

Can't seem to locate it, though.

A dark object in a night sky is impossible to see.

The sputtering of an aged pickup truck rolls by, confusing my thoughts.

I hear it stop.

It turns back.

Drives by again.

Fades into the distance. The sound slowly diving deeper into the abyss.

It was blue, and I'm not sure why that matters.

I need sleep, but I have too much energy right now. I hope it's dissipating into the air, being carried away with the sounds.

Into that abyss.

In the back of that blue truck.

The bird is chirping again.

A piece of metal hits the ground from a new direction.

My ears are perked and turning like satellites.

At least it feels like they are.

What was that?

A person.

Night staff. Walking to their car in the distance.

They don't even see me. Or maybe just don't care.

What's that?

I hear music now. Two kids on bikes, one with a boombox.

Weird.

I know that song, but can't put my finger on it.

The things unique to this hour.

'They only come out at night.' as they say.

But I wonder how I look.

Just sitting here listening.

To the sounds in the night.

Wondering what could be awake while I am awake.

There's that damn bird again.

Where the fuck are you, bird?

I will find you.

"Reef! What the fuck are you doing?"

"What?"

"What were you looking at? You tripping?"

"No, there was a bird. I was trying to -"

"A bird? Sure there was. You and your fucking birds. Let's go. Here's your chips."

But there was. I can still hear it.

Mmmmm...dill pickle.

Okay, that pill is definitely kicking in.

I can feel the sloppiness leveling off a bit.

Actually, yeah this is pretty good.

Maybe I should see if Fecma has more.

No. He said.

Patience. Give it some time, let it peak. He said.

I'm sure just one will be all I need. He said.

Just drink more booze. He said.

Plenty of that. Plenty of sloppy malt liquor. He said.

Ugggh, fuck. Fine.

This shit is still gross, and the farther down in the bottle you get, the worse it is.

This was a stupid idea. Malt liquor is stupid.

Fecma's fading on the couch again.

Should I wake him?

Nah, I should just leave him be.

He's been bugged enough for one night.

I should roll a joint.

Feeling restless.

But still lazy.

Malt liquor and mystery pill fighting inside me.

I'm kind of hoping the pill wins. I could go for a walk.

An adventure.
I just don't want to get up off of the couch.

Oh? Wait. Somebody's here.

A herd of elephants migrating down the stairs into my living room. I don't have room for elephants.

"There's was no fucking bird, dude. Ha, see? Told you they'd still be up."

"Ah. You guys *are* still up! Sweet."

"We come bearing chips and pepperoni sticks."

Fuck, look what the cat dragged in. Not elephants. I'm glad they made it back, though.

Regardless of whatever condition this is that they're in -
that we're all in.

"Of course we're still up. Only a few more hours 'til we can vote. Where'd you guys fuck off to after I headbutted Bob? You all were next."

"Ummmm, we went on an adventure."

"Yeah, but we came back to vote. To vote Bob!"

"Oh yeah, Bob. We brought you these signs. As housewarming gifts."

"Sweet, party gifts. Ha, you guys are fucked up. You don't need to vote for me. Vote for whoever the fuck you want, just glad you made it back."

"Is there more malt liquor? Haha."

"There's still lots."

"Ughhh, fuck that shit, I just want to sit down, relax, and smoke a nice joint. It's been a long night."

"That can be done, too. Give me some of those chips."

"Nice 'do, Fecma."

"Seriously, Droops. Just drop it."

"Yeah, man. Don't fuck with him."

Fecma's acting awake, but I think he's mostly sleeping with

eyes open right now. That's probably a good thing, but he's more than likely going to wake up and forget he's now bald all over again. That won't be fun. I don't want another headbutt.

We'll cross that bridge when we get there.

Maybe Fecma won't look in a mirror or touch his skull until after we vote and part our separate ways.

Not likely, though.

"I can in every way mistake the pain I feel inside.
It comes at me, evil thoughts just creepin' through my mind."

"Remember that guy on the bike?"

"Oh yeah! Haha. We should've checked to see if he was still there on our way back."

"I'm sure he is."

"That was fucked."

Yup. It was fucked.
Circling, spiraling,
into a tight nest,
and then falling asleep. Ending.
Like time. Spiraling towards our death.
Spinning ever tighter, until we get sucked down the drain.

"I can in every way feel the stress all tangled up inside.
Too blind to see the emptiness and sorrow of their lives."

I don't like it when I'm reminded that time is linear.
A snake whose back we slowly slide down
not knowing
if it's towards the head or tail.

Too minor to matter.

We all die, though.

And we all wake up with this somewhere on our minds.

"We should go back and check."
"Nah, fuck that. Leave him be."
"Yeah. Let him sleep."

"I'm gonna try. I'm gonna die."

Sleep. Death.

Either it's the gel mask we wear while we sleep to prevent the lines of aging, or it's the carefully dry-cleaned shirt in a plastic bag hanging from the doorknob, or maybe it's the sweat-stained hat used to hide a balding skull. We all choose our costumes, and wear them infinitely out into a finite environment.

We are water balloons that can be poked and spilled out into the street with the greatest of ease.

We're amazingly fragile.

Our timeline

can be severed

so easily.

"I can never break free. You wait for me, I call out to you.
Another day I'll live forever. Why?"

"Hey. Who wants to smoke a joint?"
"Fuck yeah, roll it up."

Yeah. I think I need one right about now.

"I'm going to try, but I'm going to die. I'm going to try."

"Yeah, it was fucked up. He was totally just -"

"Ugh, I'm sorry, man. I'm fucking done. I need to call it a night."

Yup, I'm done. Had to say it. Woah.

That seriously came out of nowhere.

I just got punched by an intense buzz.

They're still talking. I can't hear anything.

I'm seeing three dancing faces of whoever the fuck that is in front of me right now. Who are you? Stay still.

My stomach doesn't feel right. I'm salivating like crazy.

The more I think about how much I might puke, the more I realize how drunk I really am. So drunk. So drunk.

I've got the spins.

Over and over again.

Quicker than I want them to be.

Uncontrollably

dizzy.

They aren't really spins though,

it's more like

watching a waterfall - or rain falling - at an arc.

But I

keep focusing

on an individual pebble

of liquid

and following it

to the water's surface - quickly - and as

it splashes you

quickly

find a new one ready

to take the plunge and

follow it.

Falling, rising and falling again in this
hellish arc that
won't let you
hit the floor.
One of those rare moments where
the limbo is worse
than the hell.
At least once i finally fall
into this hell it will mean sleep.
Sleep.
Mmmmm, sleep.
Yes. That.

"What about voting, dude. I thought that was the whole point of all this."

"Fuck."

FUCK.
Fuck.
fuck.
FUCK.
Fuck.
fuck.
He's right.
He's right.
He's right.
But I
But I
But I

Can't do this
Can't do this
Can't do this
Right now.
Right now.
Right now.

Need to

Need to

Need to

Wait

Wait

Wait

For this waterfall

this waterfall

waterfall

To stop.

Stop.

STOP.

INTERMISSION

"As the polls open across the country, citizens of this great nation have already begun lining up to cast their votes. And although the weather hasn't been quite friendly over on the East Coast this morning, it hasn't stopped people from bundling up and making their voices heard. Isn't that right, Susan?"

"That's right, Tom. You can tell by the winds here that normally this wouldn't be the type of place to see so many people standing outside. But here they are - and in good spirits, no less - waiting to cast their ballot. On an important day like today, the people we've spoken to haven't at all been afraid to brave the elements in order to make their voice heard."

She read the words from the teleprompter, forgetting them as quickly as they left her mouth.

"I have Mary here with me - who I met earlier - and she's been serving free coffee and hot chocolate to the people waiting in line. All from the back of her pickup truck. Mary how does it feel to be here this morning?"

"Well, it's a historic moment. Every election is. Obviously, we were all hoping for better weather but we're used to this sort of thing around here. We just figured we'd do our part and offer some warmth to all the people coming to vote. So yeah, my sister and I decided to keep our restaurant closed for the day, and show up here instead. Just doing our part, and encouraging people to come out and make their voices heard. It's important, I think."

"That's what it's all about. Coming together as communities to vote, and encouraging other people to do the same. Thank you for taking the time to talk to us, Mary. I'll let you get back to what you were doing. This is Susan Peturovic. Reporting live."

"Thank you, Susan. Now let's go over to..."

Holy shit, what the fuck?

I think I blacked out for a while there.

So bright.

Why am I outside?

"Where are we going?"

"What? We're going to vote. Come on, Reef. Final stretch, you can do it."

Holy shit. We're actually going to vote.
We drank all night.
Straight through to the morning.
Well, mostly.
There's a lot of pieces I don't remember.
But, yeah. All-nighter.
Been a while since I've done that.
Usually once the birds start to chirp and a bit of light begins to creep through the window that's it.
If it even gets to that point.
So it must be about nine in the morning now.
Fuck.
The malt liquor was almost torture.
Trying to stay awake while drinking that shit wasn't easy.
So drunk. So tired.
Head is pounding.
Walking is hard.
I can hear my feet slapping drunkenly against the sidewalk.
I can feel each foot-slap reverb up through my skeleton and rattle my ear drums. Slap. Slap. Slap. Fuck.
It hurts my mind but I don't care.
I can barely see anything.
The whole neighbourhood is a blur.

I don't care.
It's time to vote.
Slap. Slap. Slap.
It's finally time to vote.
That was the point of this night. Vote Bob.
Slap. Slap.

Woooooooo! We did it!

I think I'm going to puke.
Not 'til I vote.

Slap. Slap. Slap.

Not until we get to the, uh...

...the voting place?

I have no idea where we are going.

"Where are we going?"
"To vote!"
"Right. But where?"
"Don't worry about it. I know where we're going."

Bob.
Right.
That guy.
Voting and shit.

Fuck, what time is it?

Slap. Slap. Slap.

Bob looked uncomfortable walking down the street.

Uncomfortable in his skin.

Shoulders tensed, and a pained expression thrown towards every vehicle that goes by.

I just met the guy, but it's pretty safe to assume,

"You don't get out much, do you Bob?"

"I try not to."

"Yeah? Why's that?"

The same pained expression - but launched inwards this time - followed by a puff from his smoke.

He thought for a quiet while before answering, keeping his eyebrows clenched like he was squinting at something in the distance.

"Do you know what I did for the millennium?"

"The millennium?"

"I went over to a friend's place - well, the motel room he was living in - and hung out with him, watching Bruce Lee flicks. It was probably about ten o'clock when I showed up there, and he didn't have any sort of way to check the time at his place.

"So - it gets to the point where - all I know is, I finally left to grab a snack. At three-thirty in the morning. I mean, I could hear a few fireworks in the distance while Bruce Lee fought Kareem Abdul Jabar, so I was vaguely aware of when the moment happened and how surreal it was, but I was separated from it. I wasn't a part of the millennium. A 'once in a dozen lifetimes' event. Passed me right by.

"Anyway. After I left, I followed drunk people as they wandered down snowy sidewalks - from a distance, completely unnoticed - just curious about where they were going. I remember one old dude in rather classy attire. He took a right turn, then another, then another, then another, then another. Simply walking around the same block over and over. I followed him for two or three laps and then I wandered onward.

"Another person, a lady, just kept walking straight. At every single intersection she would stop, look both ways, think about it for a while, and then just continue going straight.

"They were going nowhere, both those people. I was going nowhere, but at least I knew it. It was just another day for me. I don't know. The world is always trying to pretend that it is something special - that every single day matters - and if today doesn't, then tomorrow will. Me? I just see all these people walking around in circles all the time, and I don't like to be reminded of it."

"So then why hold an election party and invite people out here to vote if nothing matters?"

"Because, sometimes I really, really need to pretend that things do matter."

"In most areas of the country it looks as though we will have great weather on this election day. Unfortunately, a couple areas on the East Coast weren't so lucky and woke to strong winds and heavy rain. Thankfully though, a good Samaritan is doing his part to help people get to and from their polling stations as they deal with the strong weather. Let's go live to Greg with the story."

"Thanks, Tom. As you can see, it's quite wet out here this morning and winds have been peaking at thirty-five km/h offshore. I'm here with Jim Stratford - a local school bus driver - who decided to volunteer his time after finishing his route this morning and ferry local citizens to and from nearby polling stations. Jim, what gave you the idea to come out here this morning and help out?"

"Oh, I've been doing this for over - I don't know - thirty years

now? Since back when what's-his-name was elected. Anyway, I remember it being a pretty cold Autumn during that election. The weather had already turned around these parts so a lot of people had no way to get out to the polling station. We don't have one here - have to go the next town over - so, I figured after I had dropped the kids off at school I'd drive over to Jack's - like I normally do, for a morning coffee - and just start offering people a lift if they wanted.

"See, most of us stop in at Jack's at some point through the day. We're a pretty tight-knit community like that. People were really thankful and all that - askin' if I'd do 'er again for everyone - so I've just been offering the service ever since, I suppose. A day full of friendly faces telling stories while we take part in our great democracy. Who could complain about that?"

"Well said. Looks like a new group of people have begun to gather around your bus back there. Are you getting ready to make another journey?"

"Yeah, we're planning on leaving in seven or eight minutes. Not quite a full load, but it's enough to make the trip worth it. Some people wait a couple trips before coming back, too. So that they can get some shopping done while out there. I'm fine with it, as long as they vote."

"Good for you. Well thank you, Jim. Both for your time, and the service you're offering to the community here today."

"No problem. Thank you."

"This is Greg McMiller. Reporting live."

"Thanks for the report, Greg. Let's now go to Kim, where polls have recently opened in another part of the country. Kim, how's the energy there this morning?"

"Thanks, Susan. The energy is definitely intense here at -"

"I really appreciate you boys coming out."
"Well, it's our civic duty, right?"

I wonder what we look like to her.

Cathy.

Sitting there with her little name tag and government issued stationery.

Looking up at us from the foldout table.
Looking up at five hooligans.
Reeking of weed booze and cigarettes,
sporting metal and punk t-shirts,
unshaven and unkempt.
Not able to stand - or see - straight.
We must be quite the scene.
Fuck, I'm drunk.
Let's get this over with. I don't want to be here anymore.
The sunlight burns.

Voting.

What's the point? Our opinions don't matter. They get lost in the herd. Being here is futile. The 'X' is meaningless, but it makes people special I suppose, like they have a sense of individuality. A voice, and a -

"Name?"
"Huh?"
"Your name, sir? And are you registered to vote?"

Always sounds weird being called a 'sir'.
Catches me off guard, for some reason.

"Nope. I mean, I don't know. I'm with him."
"Okay. Well, do you have any ID with you?"

"Yup. Here you go."

The cards that prove I'm me.

Or that he's me. The guy on the card.

Whatever.

She's scanning them suspiciously. What's the issue?

Is there something wrong?

Can I not vote?

I've never done this before.

I suppose it's kind of weird that I'm completely unfamiliar with this whole process.

It's a little intimidating, though.

She reaches for a giant ledger and begins thumbing through it for my name.

I feel guilty of something.

There's a long pause.

"Nope. Okay, no problem. Was just checking if you were in the registry. We will just have to enter you in manually. It'll only take a moment. If I could just get you to go see those people at the table over there."

No.

No, I don't want to see those people at the table over there.

"Sure."

I did it.

I voted.

It feels weird.

Like, the first time having sex.

Quiet, awkward, and not nearly as exciting as expected.

A whole night of foreplay for that, eh?

Not worth it.

Ha, and here I am having a smoke.

Waiting for everyone else to finish.

Premature ejaculation.

What?

Fuck, I need sleep so bad.

My mind is slipping.

I should -

ummmmm.

I should wait.

Wait and see if Spudley's planning on heading back with me.

Yeah.

What a night.

I really, really needed that.

I must say, it has really taken my mind off of things.

So many things.

I can feel those things waiting at the door - waiting for me to open it and let them back in - but I think they're more than comfortable spending a bit more time out in the yard.

It's a nice morning. They'll be fine.

Yeah. I'll tend to my demons later, after some sleep.

I'm not sure how I should feel right now.

Bob.

Bob surely can't win, right?

There's no way that random groups of misfits across the country have turned up in droves to draw an 'X' next to an unknown individual and let him lead the country.

No fucking way.

In all honesty though, I care so little about politics that I don't even know who Bob was running against. I barely remember the other candidates' names, and couldn't even repeat them to you if you asked me, even though I just saw them printed in type not ten minutes ago.

Curious.

I wish I would've been paying attention earlier in the election. I still feel rather uninformed about everything that has just happened. What just happened? I voted. Right.

Voting. So weird.

Ah, Droops is done.

Here he comes.

"Aren't they supposed to give you a sticker after voting?"

"Nah, not here."

"Damn. Whatever. Can I get a smoke?"

"Yup, here."

"Thanks. They'll be out soon. We were thinking of going for breakfast and then calling it a night. Or, day. Whatever."

"Hmmm, alright. I really need sleep, but my body will probably thank me if I eat something first. We'll walk back up to Bob's and I'll drive us."

"Drive? You good to drive?"

"At this point? Yes, and no. Besides, when did that ever bother you? Here they come."

"So, what's the plan?"

"Walk back to your place, and then Reef's going to drive us to get some grub."

"Sounds good. Let's do this."

"There's only one thing to do at a time like this. Strut."

I know we all probably look like hell right now, but I feel great. We aimed to stay up all night and be amongst the first people in town to cast our votes.

We did.

We fulfilled our civic duty.

Fuck yeah.

Almost makes me want to walk around town with a smug expression reminding other people to vote, or asking them if they've voted yet.

Just so that people know that I indeed already have.

I wanted a damn sticker.

Didn't get fuck all.

Bullshit.

Even the dentist gives you something afterward.

I guess that's done as more of an apology though, for knowingly causing pain and discomfort.

The government never apologizes, or admits fault.

Whatever.

None of this is going to matter, though.

It doesn't change anything.

Nothing has changed during our entire lives. Why the fuck would it suddenly change now, like magic? That just isn't the way politics work. It's such a slow, drawn out process. We won't ever see any sort of genuine change, just a different face progressing towards the same old interests at a slow enough rate so that no one knows it's happening.

People always want to get from point A to point B faster, but if you find a way to shoot them there in seconds they'll complain about how uncomfortable the journey was. You can't win. Especially when you have more and more people with their own unique ways of complaining if change is implemented too quickly, or too slowly even.

There's a pace that must be maintained, a perfect medium. The 'room temperature' of progression. If it gets too hot or too cold - too fast or too slow - it causes discomfort.

And because of that, nothing is going to change. It will merely take on the perception of change, just enough as to keep people content with the idea that we are indeed moving forward.

We aren't.

This is another day like any other, and when it is over the next one will follow.

"Fuck, Droops. Hurry up."

"I'm coming. Was just lost in thought."

"Yeah, well I'm hungry."

We were all hungry.

My brain couldn't even process thoughts until I stuck a piece of bacon in my face and chased it with some coffee.

Ah, food.

Felt like it took forever to get to Bob's and then here.

Meat.

Salt.

And grease.

So good.

I left my body until this food arrived.

"Why did we do this again?"

"So that we would vote."

"Yeah, but," my brain still hurts, "don't we have all day to do that still?"

"Face it. We would have never gone if we didn't do it this way. I know I wouldn't have fuckin' voted."

Fecma's right.

And I think Bob knew this all along. Strange guy. His plate arrived but he didn't even touch it, instead got up and went outside. I can see him through the glass, smoking. Might as well take the chance to ask.

"So, what's with Bob?"

"What do you mean?"

"Well, how did you guys meet him I guess?"

"Fuck, how did I meet Bob? I knew about him in high school, I guess. He was 'the guy who smoked joints like cigarettes' among people in the smoking pit who didn't know him, haha. He laughed when I told him that years later. But anyway, I don't know really. I think I ran into him in the smoking pit one day during my spare and he invited me back to his place for a toke since we both had time to kill. The high school was right around the corner from his parent's place. So, it was really convenient. I started going to his place at lunch hour to get high while his folks were at work. I don't know, I guess we just sort of hit it off and it led to drinking together. He moved here from somewhere but I can't remember the place. Why?"

"I don't know, he's just - he's a different sort of character, I guess. I mean, I've never seen anyone handle a raging drunk - like your ass, Fecma - the way he did. It was like he wanted you to hurt him."

"Yeah, that's Bob. I don't know. He just sort of goes with the flow."

"And he's never shied away from pain."

"Yeah. The way I see it, Spudley. Bob's just really comfortable with who he is."

"Hmmmm, I've never heard it put that way but it kind of makes sense. Yeah. 'Comfortable with who he is.' That's a good way of putting it. Interesting."

"I wouldn't put too much thought into it. Basically, he's just a good guy to know. I'm surprised you haven't met him before."

"Yeah, me too."

We sat there sponging up egg yolk with toast while the nation rose from their slumber to choose its new voice.

I was more concerned with the Bob that stood outside the

glass, though.

Smoking, and thinking about something.

So, we voted.

Still trying to fake interest.

Trying to convince myself that it matters.

Whatever.

It was a good night.

Mission accomplished.

If we weren't this drunk we never would have voted.

There's no way our sober minds could've been convinced to make the journey. No way to trick ourselves that there was any sense of purpose to the task without copious amounts of sedatives.

Needed to trick the logic centers.

Induce a suggestive state.

The type of state that causes a person to lose control of the helm and slip into 'auto-pilot mode'. Yelling and fighting and singing and hugging. Puking and drinking and puking some more, walking and stumbling and falling and getting back up and falling again.

The type of state that can leave a person in a drunk tank - bloodied and broke - if ever noticed by anyone outside the confines of where such behaviour is acceptable.

The type of state that makes you think shaving your buddy's head is a good idea. Fuck, that was stupid.

It's only at that point that a stupid, penciled 'X' inside a circle makes any sort of sense at all.

This was a victory by unconventional means.

I guess I knew that all along, in an unspoken way.

Maybe that was my plan the whole time.

Well, I know that was my plan, but I guess I didn't see the big picture as well as my subconscious did.

You can never quite anticipate whether a plan will work or not, but I think throughout the night I grew surer and more prepared than any of us for the inevitable outcome.

I mean, without Bob we wouldn't have voted today.

I don't mean me.

I mean 'Bob'.

We would've procrastinated through the afternoon, and made excuses to anyone who would've asked us if we'd voted yet, saying that we planned on doing it later.

Letting other things step in the way until the deadline had safely passed and we could provide a sufficient excuse as to not knowing where that time went.

I know it. That's what I would've done.

That's what we all would've done.

That's what we do when faced with opportunity.

But not today.

Today it's ten-thirty in the morning and I'm having a smoke, while everyone else is struggling to create motor functions.

Chewing and swallowing a greasy breakfast

in an empty diner.

After already voting.

I'm not sure how I should feel.

I feel good?

I guess?

I'm trying to care.

To care about the fact that I voted, but right now I'm more concerned with how badly they screwed up my over-easy eggs.

...and that I drank Granger's piss.

I should eat,
but food still isn't appetizing to me at the moment.

Too aware of my insides...

Fuck!

I think I'm sobering up.
That's what it is.
That's what I'm feeling.
I hate sobering up while still awake.
Fuck this.

I need to go back in, try and finish my breakfast, and get home to bed.

Fuck, I'm tired.

"As the red fades from your wrinkled dress,
a picture of the people you've impressed
Hangs on a wall above you..."

"You going to eat your toast?"

"Nah, take it."

"Sweet. Thanks."

"Well, I'm going to drive Spudley home and then go crash. Fecma, you need a lift anywhere?"

"I'm good. I'll just wander home from here after I settle up."

"You sure?"

"Yeah, man."
"Alright, cheers. 'Twas fun, and all that jazz."
"Yeah, have a good one."
"Cheers."
"Cheers."
"Oh, Bob. I'll probably swing by later on after some sleep."
"Yeah, sounds good."
"Alright, we're out."
"Peace."

I watch them pay at the counter and leave while I'm spreading peanut butter across Spudley's abandoned toast.

Add some jam.

Love me these little packets.

I've got a shitload of 'em at home but that's not going to slow me from pocketing all the ones left in this dish.

Free peanut butter,
jam,
honey,
hot sauce,
ketchup,
mustard.
Condiments.

I have a little basket dedicated to them.

Soy sauce is weird, though.

Turns to glass if you keep it for too long.

But, man. Honey.

Honey packs are the best. Pure gold.

They last forever.

"...fingers stretched across your empty gaze..."

"So. Had a really weird thing happen to me the other day."
"Yeah? What happened?"

I look up from my thoughts and let Bob elaborate,

"I don't know how to explain it. It was a really weird feeling. Like - well, you know how you have that voice inside your head? You know. That sort of internal dialogue - or whatever, like - 'Hmm, I'm hungry.' or 'I wonder what time it is'. You know? The filter or thought process or whatever before an idea comes straight out of your mouth, right?"

"Yup, I get it."

"Well, it was like that voice inside my head - for no apparent reason - started yelling all of a sudden. It just started fucking yelling. And not like it was yelling at me. It was just filtering my thoughts with a full on fucking scream. Like 'HMMMM, I'M HUNGRY.' And it was really fucked up. Really, really fucked up. But then I couldn't even stop it. I was just sitting there at home - alone - with my thoughts going 'WHY ARE DOING THIS? THIS MAKES NO SENSE.' and no matter what my thoughts were, even if they were 'THIS ICE CREAM IS AMAZING' they would come out like that. Like an angry yell inside my own head. I don't know if that makes any sense. It's just the only way I know how to explain it. First time it's ever happened to me. I don't know. It was fucked. Anything like that ever happen to you?"

Fuck. Yes.

I could tell it was taking him a lot of focus to try and describe what he was talking about. But, yes. I knew exactly what he meant. I just never knew how to articulate it myself. My internal dialogue got angry a lot, and for no reason.

Yes.

I knew *exactly* what he fucking meant.

I get that shit all the time.

Fuck.

"All the time, man. All the fucking time."

"Shit. Really? That was seriously the one and only time in my life that it's ever happened. Got me kind of curious if other people experience it. Dude. That sucks. That shit was fucked."

"You don't even know."

"So, how do you make it go away?"

"I don't know. It just goes away on its own after a while."

"Strange. Yeah, that's fucked up shit. So weird. But, I'm going to head home. Hey, Fecma. You forgot the marmalade."

"Fuck that, I never take the marmalade. But yeah, cheers. Have a good one, man."

"Cheers."

"And the evening waits,
while you get caught up to your own mistakes..."

I imagine marmalade is the only type of jam you'd get in jail.
But yeah, sleep.
Sleep seems like a good idea.
I'm outta here, too.

"...made up of different lies I wouldn't want to have in my mind."

So
very
tired.
So very
home. Finally.
Thank fuck. My
parents
aren't here.

In no mood - or condition - for conversation right now.
That's for sure.

And thank fuck
for Reef driving me home.
For everything lately, really.

Fading
so very fast.

A slice of processed cheese and then

triple-check the locks

and alarm
clocks. Before retiring.

Routine.

The day is looking at me from windows already. No.
Too

soon.

It's still night.
Until I wake.

My own moon
and sun.

Punctual.
Slip
into something more comfortable.
Becoming predictable,

Donnie Boy, time to...

No, Mom.

I can't wake up yet.

Not until I sleep.

Damn. What a night.

Everyone else is home. I can finally go crash, too.

Fuck. I forgot about this stupid window.

I hate climbing through this damn thing.

My ribs are seriously bruised from this damn sill.

Uggggh, fuck. Fuckin-

"Ow! Fuck!"

"Reef? What the fuck are you doing?"

Oh, shit.

Shitshitshitshitfuck.

Talk about being caught with my hand in the cookie jar.

She's staring at me. From inside.

This wasn't how I wanted this to go down.

"Jodi? Ummm, I can explain. Just -"

"What the fuck? Just use the fucking door! You're going to break my window sill. Fuck."

Right. If she's here I can just use the -

"Right, sorry. One second."

Shit. She's here.

She's here.

I'm not ready for this right now.
Fuck. What do I do?
Still drunk.
Mind is drawing a blank.
Putting the pencil down, raising arms in defeat.
No words.
I can barely even walk properly.
Not much choice at this point.
Go around to the door and just go in.
One foot in front of the other.
You can do this.

Seriously. Not now.
I need to focus.
Stairs are hard.
I did it.
Ummm.
She's just staring at me, confused...

"Jodi - ummmm - hey. It's not what it looks like. I -"

"Looks like you were climbing through my window. And that you've been squatting here for a while. In your own filth. By candlelight. What the fuck, Reef?"

"Okay, so maybe it's exactly what it looks like. I was going to tell you. I mean, but I just - I didn't know how to get a hold of you. I figured you'd eventually be back here and so I - it's right here - I have a joint rolled and everything, and I figured I could explain everything that's happened and -"

"Woah. Reef, calm down. It's okay. It's cool. I just - actually, I didn't expect it to be you who was squatting here. I thought it was Droops - or maybe Yunk - but not you. I've been here a couple times, I could tell that someone had been coming in. I'm not mad. It's all good. Just, well. Dude."

"Yeah, hey. It's me. Sorry."

"It's all good. What's going on, Reef? Did your Dad kick you out or something?"

"My Dad? Well, actually. I - ummm... my Dad's dead."

"Oh, fuck. Seriously?"

"Yeah, seriously. Heart attack."

"Sorry. I'm really sorry. Ah, shit. Reef. That sucks. Reef. What happened? I mean, you don't have to tell me if you don't want to but -"

"It's okay. Happened at work. He died on the way to the hospital."

"Brutal. Fuck, dude. Reef. Fuck. You okay?"

"I am now. If you asked a few days ago I couldn't have looked you in the eye and said the same thing, but yeah. I've struggled, I've - well, I'm here but - umm, yeah. Anyway. Let's smoke that joint?"

"Yeah, Reef. For sure. Listen. Shit, stay here as long as you want. I've got this place leased for the rest of the month and if you need more time after that I can -"

"No, no. It's okay. I'll have things figured out by then. I promise. I appreciate it, though."

"Alright. Well. Shit. Okay. Sorry, but can I ask a favour?"

"Yeah, no worries. What is it?"

"Nevermind. It can wait."

We've both spent time running from things.

The silence grew awkward. Thankfully she broke it.

Thank fucking God.

"Fuck, this is some good weed. Can you get more of this?"

"Actually, yeah I can. But - sorry - I've been up all night and can barely think right now."

"No worries. Actually, I just wanted to grab a few things to bring over to Mel's."

"Yeah? How are you and Mel doing?"

"She fucks me good."

"Yeah. You would say that, you crazy dyke."

"Hey, hey. I resent that. I'll fuck anything. I've fucked enough of your friends even."

"And that's why I stopped bringing them around. You'll fuck anything with legs. What's that called again? Not bisexual, the sleeps-with-anything one."

"Pansexual."

"Sure. That one."

I still think there must be an even dirtier word for what she is. One not yet defined by Webster's dictionary. Whatever. I smoked the joint, and told the pansexual with witch nipples what had been going on lately.

I told her everything.

It felt good to get it all out.

When she hugged me before leaving, I swear I felt her extra nipples against my lower ribs...

and now I can't sleep.

So tired.

Need sleep.

You ever have a moment where a song plays in your head?

And I don't mean - like - a song by a band you know. I mean an original, never-been-played-by-human-beings type of song.

Has your brain ever written its own songs?

Mine has, and there's no way to play them on instruments.

I could never map them on sheets of music.

I have no idea how to make that music physical.

It's not even my ears listening. It's all in the mind.

It's faint, but it's there. It is, but it isn't.

But I guess that's the point.

It's not meant to 'be'.

That's my music.

My song.

For me alone. Not meant to be constructed, only heard.

I wish I could share it, but I know I can't.

It's playing right now and stuck in a loop,

putting a soundtrack behind my thoughts.

Easy to add lyrics to - and melodies - but
no point trying to share.
The moment would be lost.
The totality is simply impossible to express.
I want to record it.
How can I do that?

I can't.

But, there must be a way.
Need sleep.
Such a long night,
day,
whatever.

It's weird to think about. The world is waking - or already awake - and I'm finally submitting to sleep. Sleep always wins - and I like letting it - but when I wake up there will be a new leader of this country. Power will have changed hands.

I'm trying, but I can't wrap my head around what that will mean. Too detached from it all.

Detached, because as much as I try to, I just don't really care.

It affects me - I know - but at the same time it really doesn't.

I'm not going to wake up someone new - the way the country will - and just because the country wakes up with a new representative, it doesn't mean that it's going to truly affect me in any way.

Never has before.

I don't see why this time around should possibly be
any different.
Nothing really changes.
Nothing makes a difference.
It's just another day. Right?

At the same time, I know I think this because I want to be proven wrong.

...and the beat goes on.

FADE TO BLACK
(Again.)

Too many people.
Walking. Marching
Towards something,
but it feels more like they're walking away.

Fists pumping through the air, chest flared out, words in bold fonts across their t-shirts yelling
in between teeth clenched tight.

Ready to fight, ready to lash out like a fist from the mouth.
Alien.

Where are they going?
What are all these people walking towards?
They're walking the wrong way.
It feels like
the wrong way
but.
Everything is telling me to turn and walk with them.
Everything but my mind.
My mind says this is wrong.
That I should struggle up stream.
Against the current.
Agenda.
What?
Fight it.
Push forward like a salmon.

Why do they do it? What draws them? What force of nature makes them go where nature itself tells them not to?

I see a tree.

A willow tree, upstream through the watery crowd now like boulders on a shallow creek.

Shade.
And deep water beneath its roots.
Elbows out.
Head down.
Fight my way through

the crowd
the rocks
the boulders and current.
Affairs.
What?
Adjust.
Trajectory.
And drift.
Towards.
The willow tree.
With arms reaching over the creek, but no -
not arms
no creek
the current rises
the shores thicken
water deepens
it's not a tree
I see
It's he.

Wait. Here he is. I see him. I see Bob. I see...
He's speaking. What is he saying? What is he -
No. It's not him, it's me.
I'm talking. I'm -

I'm speaking to me...

"We are the sheep BAHH we are the mass herd born to the herd raised within forced to dwell within a colourless environment which raises us in the opinions of our kindred elders some complain it is hard to see through the herd to the outside they're assured only herd is there to be seen says the Shepherd there is nothing else to see worth seeing mass upon mass of clones chasing blind the tail the ass of the one in front of us something to do constantly jumping and stepping over others moving ahead to find more sheep falling back to sheep again no end no beginning to the sick repetitive rat race running racing attempting to beat someone hoof to the eye to win a prize never conformed to exist never ever but made to believe just around the corner it does the prize the reward for all the hard work subjected subconsciously over ourselves all this time the great the prize is death. Don't run so fast. Don't obey. WAKE UP!"

I do.

Morning?

Reality invades my thoughts and murmuring voices grow in the distance.

Get out of my head. No.

Get out of bed.

Walk towards the sound.

Shake my fist from the porch at the disturbance...

"It will still be some time before the numbers truly start showing up in the West, but at this point it's safe to say that the Alternative Party is looking at a majority government."

"Indeed. Startling results, to say the least. This is an unprecedented moment in this country's political history."

"So what does this mean?"

"Well, at this point we can still only speculate, but what we can expe-."

Droops is watching TV. What's going on?

"What's going on?"

"Bob won. Bob fucking won. You - we - we won, dude."

Wait, what? Election. Right.

Bob.

The real world.

Bob won.

Bob won?

"He won? Seriously?"

"Well, not officially. But check this shit out. Look at these numbers. This is fucked."

Checking.

Looking.

Yes, this is definitely fucked.

They're showing the map in real time as the numbers get confirmed across the country.

The entire East is black with Bob victories.

Blanketed completely.

What the fuck is going on?

As the shadow sweeps across the land specks of colour show up and disappear along with updated figures in active ridings - twinkling across the landscape - but the darkness is overwhelming.

Even with polls still open in the West there is no way they will be able to shine a light back across and fight this shadow.

The way it looks just doesn't seem right.

It's ominous, but I don't know why.

On the surface I feel like I should be happy, and that I should be looking forward to the political landscape finally being altered after a lifetime of complaining about it and wishing for change, but...

Something about this isn't sitting right with me.

No. Something is definitely wrong. I feel more like we have all just been victim to a massive deception, and once we reach the point of the reveal there isn't a single person who is going to be happy. Well, there will be happy people. I'm sure those at the root of what's going on are ecstatic with the results. But I have a feeling that no one I know personally is going to like what the future has in store.

We just elected a person we've never met. We have given our entire political system to an entity that we know nothing about. I guess no one worried about it that much because they never believed it would happen, but it has. We're looking at it. The mushroom cloud has exploded in the distance and we know that we're in the blast zone blindly waiting for the shockwave to reach us. No point in running. What's done is done.

I don't know what to expect, but it can't be good. My gut tells me this is very, very, very, not good.

You ever get that feeling like you're being handed a trophy

and probably shouldn't be? Well, something about everything happening right now just isn't sitting right, at all.

This isn't a win for the little guy.

Night is falling.

Enter the 'Age of Bob'.

Wake up.

"Hi, Mrs. Spudley. Is Donovan here?"

"Oh. Hi, Paul! Yes, we were just finishing dinner. One second, I'll go get him. Oh and Paul, we're so sorry to hear about your Dad's -"

"Thank you, Mrs. Spudley. It's appreciated. I'd rather not - well, you know."

"Oh, sorry. I didn't mean to bring up - Okay, I'll go get him for you."

It's odd. That didn't cut the way it has been lately.

Kind of grazed over me.

No.

Not odd. Just - new.

I hope it doesn't make me a bad person, but I have to admit that I kind of like it.

Like...

like a hole in my boat has been patched.

No.

Patched is the wrong word.

Patched implies duct tape and good intentions.

Right. My boat has been fixed.
Repaired.
And I don't have to stand guard with the bucket as often.
No, not often. Ever.
That bucket can rust through at this point.
For all I care.
This here vessel is sea-worthy again.
And it feels good to be able to say that.

Even if I don't quite believe it one hundred percent. Yet.

"Hey Reef, what's up?"

Right, Spudley.
Zoned out on my boat for a moment there.

"Hey, want to go for a cruise?"
"Just finishing dinner, actually. What's up?"

He closes the door and steps on the porch, in privacy.
He always was a sly one.

"Well. Want to make a sale? Long story short, the lesbian chick came home today. She's back at the place right now."

"Who?"

"Jodi. Witch tits. The chick's house I'm squatting at."

"Oh, right. Shit, she's back? Everything all good?"

"Yeah, totally. No - nothing to worry about - she's chill. But yeah, she wants a half."

"Okay. Well. Ummm. Give me like fifteen minutes? To finish eating and get ready? I'll be back out in a bit."

"Yeah, for sure. I'll just run and grab smokes and then wait out front. No rush. Need anything from the store?"

"Nah, I'm good."

"Alright. I'll see you in a bit?"

"For sure. Fifteen minutes. Cheers."

Stupid TV.

This is a strange feeling.
The winner has been decided, but -
we still have no idea who it is.

And behind this curtain...

The TV screens keep flashing back and forth from the perspective of various losers, but there are no cameras where the winning party is. Where the real party is.

Shut the fuck up, pundits.
Who won?
We know, but we don't know.

Nobody is cheering and smiling. No one is giving a victory speech. There are no celebratory bottles of wine being opened. No balloons or confetti.

Nothing.

No winner, just the faces of losers.

I think that's why this feels so odd.

There's no perspective of winning being portrayed right now, just an entire country that lost while the unknown winners celebrate in private.

This doesn't feel right.

This is not what you want to see happening within a democratic society, even if we did choose it fair and square.

This is too much right now.

I can't think about it.

Hungry. Food.

"Fuck, turn this off, I'm ordering some pizza."

"Pizza? Hmmm. I'll pitch in."

"Alright, but just warning you: I'll only agree to meat options as acceptable toppings. No veggies. Oh, but I'm cool with mushrooms or olives. They don't count as vegetables."

"Pineapple?"

"Never pineapple. Never. Never ever."

"But it's a frui-"

"Pineapple is kryptonite to pizza. Fucking poison. I feel sorry for any pizza that pineapple comes in contact with. Such a beautiful creature doesn't deserve such humilia-"

"Okay, cool. Whatever. No pineapple. That's all you had to say."

"Besides, who puts fruit on a pizza? Fucki-"

"No pineapple. I get it. Fuck, just shut up already. The basic pepperoni, bacon and 'shrooms?"

"Perfect. And extra sauce?"

"Fine. Cool. Whatever. But you need to see a shrink about your pineapple problems. Seriously."

"Pineapple is fu-"

"Yes, fine. I get it. I'll go order it from the payphone. Just settle down. I'll be back in a bit."

No. I will not settle down. I have to defend myself.

Against the pineapple.

To the death.

In honour of pizza...

Pineapple is not a topping.

My head is swimming with new ideas now.

I've never had any interest in politics before but now -

Oh, man.
Now I need to know more.

I needed this.

I needed something else to think about.
I just wish that I could make sense of it all.

Something is going on right now, but it's so much bigger than me. There's so much to take in. So much I need to catch up on.

I'm just a person.
One single person. What could I possibly do?
Why should I possibly bother doing anything?
Bob was right. Ha, Bob. Fuckin' Bob.
I wonder what he thinks about all of this right now.
He's probably still asleep.
He probably has no idea what's happening right now.
That he won.

Wish I could sleep right now.

But seriously, my thoughts will keep bouncing around inside my head unless I share them.

These new thoughts, new ideas.
Spudley might know what to do.

How to make sense of it all.
Hopefully.

Ah. Here he comes.

We should drive out to the marsh.
Yeah, the marsh.
That's a good idea.
Haven't been there in
- well -
too long.

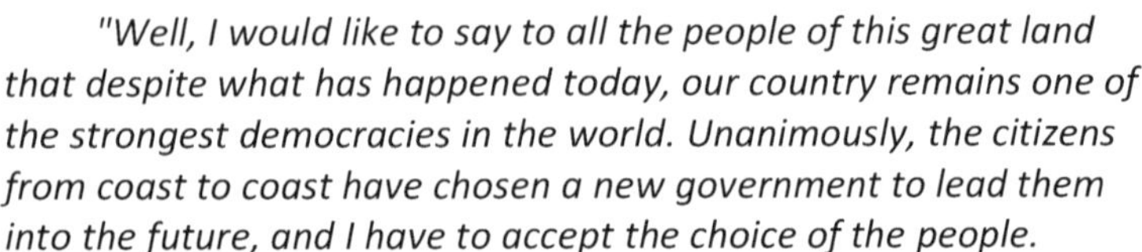

"Well, I would like to say to all the people of this great land that despite what has happened today, our country remains one of the strongest democracies in the world. Unanimously, the citizens from coast to coast have chosen a new government to lead them into the future, and I have to accept the choice of the people.

"Thank you, everybody. Merci beaucoup. It has been a pleasure to serve, and it has been a gratifying and humbling experience to again meet the people that make up this great country and shake their hands - meet their families - from one coast to the other during this campaign. We definitely put in an honest fight and stood by our beliefs. We gave everything we had to give, and there isn't a single regret to be had. How could there be? Today is a day of celebration, as citizens of the greatest country on Earth.

"We all deserve to feel a sense of happiness and optimism during this moment. While tonight's result was certainly not the one we had aimed for, the people are never wrong. The public has elected an entirely new government; a result that we accept without hesitation. I will assure our new Prime Minister of my full cooperation during the transition in these coming months, and I look forward to meeting him, and shaking his hand.

"I also want to extend my congratulations to the other party leaders and their efforts on their own campaigns respectively. It was well fought, and no one came out truly defeated here.

"To all our citizens of every stripe, across the spectrum, I salute you. Your efforts today helped keep our democracy strong. The record amount of you who came out to the polls and voted is an inspiring thing to witness and be a part of. Never forget that due to your efforts our country stands tall today, and we have built a democracy that's stronger than ever. We have -"

I wonder if he believes anything he is saying right now,

because I definitely don't.

Who writes this shit?

Fuck.

I was waiting to hear his speech.

I never use this stupid radio.

Wanted to know if he had anything enlightening to say about what just happened - who this Bob character is who now runs the fucking country - but this guy's never even met him either. He just fucking said it.

So here we are: a whole country, waiting to find out what happens next. Watching. Listening. Tuning in.

Waiting for this man who we've come to know over the past few years to explain what the fuck is going on, and he's as clueless as the next guy.

Just, "Blah, blah-blah-blah, Bob's your uncle."

Bob's our uncle.

Holy shit.

...and behind door number three...Uncle Bob.

Congratulations?

I'd like to say it's a vague analogy but fuck, it's eerily accurate. He's not the father, or mother, or any level of blood relative. He has married his way into the political family.

Blood by law.

Bob has become family, legally, and has to be accepted as such by everyone around him. This new character who you can't relate to personally because you don't know him too well.

Because he's new. And because...

He isn't blood.

But you have to accept him as such. Let him come to the holiday meals with full clearance to participate and allow him to get involved in the gift exchange and family portraits.

If he makes children, those children will be blood. Forever merged in a primordial communion. And him as well.

But who is he?

Is he a crazy uncle? You never know with an uncle. Uncles are unpredictable by nature. Maybe it won't last long. Maybe they'll get a divorce - and he'll be forgotten as quickly as he was introduced - but for now, he's here and he's family.

Yup, Bob is our uncle now.

This is a weird feeling.

I need a drink.

I should head downstairs for a couple brews. I'm sure they've got the news on in the bar right now. Bunch of drunks yelling at each other about politics. Should be fun.

Might get to bounce a drunkard or two, which is definitely a fun way to pay the tab.

Tab. Beer.

Yeah, fuck sitting in this box.

Let's go.

Ah, fuck. My fucking head. Fuckin' -

It feels weird not having hair.

Fucking Bob, seriously.

Hmmmm.

Where's my toque?

If I throw it on maybe people won't ask me why I shaved my fucking head. I fucking didn't. I can just picture it too, drunks harassing me all night long...

"Why'd yuh shave yer 'ead?"

"I didn't."

"Pffft. Yea yuh did. Ain't no hair there on yer 'ead no more."

"Just shut the fuck up."

"But yuh def'nitely -"

"Just shut the fuck up."

Yup. Getting angry. Need booze.

"...all along the broadening skies. under the every light i will lie scratching, claw, and grip the rails. Sigh. Everyday my living hell."

"What are you doing?"

"Listening to some Blind Melon, putting things on shelves. What does it look like I'm doing?"

"...get me out of here, get me out of here, get me out of here."

"Yeah, but, an empty forty of Olde English? On display?"

"Yeah. I'm going to build a bottle shelf for all the different varieties and types of empties."

"Okay. Why?"

"Hey, I like to daze away to a place no one has known.
In a state of mind I could call mine, and only I could own"

"Why? Because I don't have things. But I figure these things have memories. Sure, I could return the glass for ten cents or whatever, but I like the idea that when I look at this particular bottle on this shelf here that I will remember random moments from last night. Years down the road. If that makes sense."

"Actually, it does. So, are you going to grab a random bottle from all the types in the kitchen?"

"Now, you see? They're watching everything I say and they're watching everything I do."

"Nah, that would be cheating. I'd put the piss bottle on the shelf, but you said Granger smashed it. I really should stop ignoring that room and deal with all that bullshit in there. Thanks for fucking reminding me."

"Hey, not my fault. I was just trying to pass you a joint and you went all OCD."

"Sometimes I ask myself, I ask, 'Why am I even here?'"

"Can't help it. This is my place now, I need to make it truly mine. It's consuming me."

"Yes, you're Bob and you have won supremacy over your domain. I get it."

"Exactly. I must redecorate. My energy is through the fucking roof right now. I had some crazy dreams. Still trying to remember what they were."

"Yeah, dreams are weird. Did I ever tell you that I had a dream once that lasted an entire month?"

"Nope. Wait. What do you mean? Same dream for a whole month? That's kind of odd."

"No. I mean one dream. One night. One month worth of experience. All at once."

"Really? Okay, now that's fucked up."

"Oh, it definitely fucked me up. Like, I was this prisoner in a sort of *Oh, Brother Where Art Thou?* style prison; if you know what I mean?"

"Never seen it, but I get what you're saying. Stripey shirts and chain gang shit."

"Exactly. Okay, so yeah. We would go out and work on the chain gang, actually. For real. It sucked. I remember sweating my ass off, and burning under the sun. Back in the prison, I would eat when meals were served. I remember feeling hungry. And tired, and sore, and all the things a person feels. I remember the food and what it tasted like. I would sleep when I was tired and then wake up the next morning still within the dream, within the prison, within this foreign body. It was fucked. I even remember shaving, and it was really weird because I could see myself, and I was old. I had grey stubble that folded on itself inside of wrinkles along my face. I remember what I *looked* like. For quite a few years I even remembered my name, and always wanted to try and look it up and see if that person ever existed. I've forgotten it over the years, though. Kinda sucks."

"Won't you stop watching me? I said they're watching me, watching me, watching me."

"That's fucked, dude. I've never heard of that before."

"Like I said. It messed with me. I mean, imagine being an eight year old kid and having a dream like that. I spent a month in a shitty prison, doing hard labour. My cellmate planned an escape which failed and I remember him getting shot and falling into my arms and dying. Fuck, I remember crying and shit as the life washed from his eyes, and mourning him for days. Not eating, not shaving. And then, out of nowhere I woke up.

"I suddenly had to remember all over again that I was an eight year old kid who needed to get dressed and eat some breakfast before going to school. But, yeah. That happened. And I have no fucking clue what it means."

"And they ripped away my memories and I can't remember who I was before."

"Me neither. I've never had a dream like that, man."

"I've never had one like it since. It was the one and only time. Not sure if I'd want to go through that again, but I'd like to know more about what the fuck happened to me that night. It sucks that it's been so long and I've forgotten most of the details. I used to remember."

"Dreams are weird. That's all I know. I remember a beach, and maybe a cliff-side with trails coming down it like ant farm tunnels, but that's about it. Whatever. This Bob shit, though. Kind of feels like I'm still dreaming."

"Yeah. I don't quite know what to make of all this. Fuck it. Out of our hands now."

"I guess so."

"...and I wonder."

The marsh is so quieting.

Quiets the mind, and allows the thoughts to speak in turn. An organized meeting of ideas, under a set agenda, unlike the normal. The busy intersection with a single crossing guard trying to maintain order.

Order doesn't need to be maintained here.

The mind has space to stretch out - without interference - across the marsh, and into the dark channels between islands of bulrushes.

The silhouettes of ducks drift by occasionally. Silent against an orange backdrop cast into the sky by the halogen glow from fields of glass houses in the distance.

It is forever sunset here.

Forever a moment between two times.

Frozen in place through the dark hours that surround it.

The dark world beyond.

In such an overpopulated world, I always find it strange that more people don't escape to these places that exist in between things. Like the spaces between words, or the gaps between songs.

These things are important.

Without them, there is no room to breathe.

No room to react.

To reflect.

No moment to separate one time from the next.

The spaces between moments are moments themselves, and in that place is where I like to sit sometimes.

To gather my thoughts.

Make some sense out of all these fragments.

"You're awful quiet tonight."

"Yeah, sorry man. Tired. Tried to get some sleep earlier but had too much on my mind so I ended up spending the day at the library. On the computers. A lot going on in my head right now. I like to come out here and think. Sort out my thoughts."

"Okay. Well, what's up?"

"Hmmmm. Trying to figure out how to say it, or where to begin. Basically - well, I guess - well, the big thing is...hmmmm...I found Bob."

"Bob?"

"Robert Blytheswood. The Bob representing our riding. The local 'Bob' that is part of the new Prime Minister Bob's party whose house we drove out to and it didn't exist. I'm close to finding out what his real name is. Where he actually lives."

"Okay. So? I don't really know what that means."

"I'm not sure if I do either, but I know it means something, and I can't shake this feeling like I have to do something about it."

"Like what?"

"I don't know. Which is I guess why we're here."

A heron cuts through the air with perfect silence and I've completely forgotten the specifics of what we were talking about, instead plunging back into the fragments of information that need assembling. I feel like I need to do something but I'm waiting for someone to tell me what that something is.

I guess first I need to find out who that someone is.

No.

I know who that someone is.

It's me.

And I know what I want to do...

I want to kill Bob.

END SCENE. CUT TO CREDITS.

SONGS REFERENCED:

PG.3 - THE JIMI HENDRIX EXPERIENCE - HEY JOE
PG.93 - SKINNY PUPPY - WORLOCK
PG.141 - METALLICA - ENTER SANDMAN
PG.145 - RUSTY - GROOVY DEAD
PG.150 - DAYS OF THE NEW - WHAT'S LEFT FOR ME
PG.170 - BURZUM - EA, LORD OF THE DEEP
PG.183 - CLUTCH - 7 JAM
PG.195 - MARILYN MANSON - KINDERFELD
PG.198 - YOB - UNIVERSE THROB
PG.204 - KORN - PREDICTABLE
PG.225 - TREBLE CHARGER - RED
PG.249 - BLIND MELON - I WONDER

ALSO BY JAIMEN SHIRES:

Every bird has a story.

Have you ever watched a Crow eat crackers?

Have you seen a Quail's topknot bounce around while it runs, or considered what the life of a headless Chicken is like, or imagined the flavour of Flamingo meat?

I have.

Bird Droppings: A Collection of Avian Anecdotes collects over fifty wildly-varying tales in regards to birds.

Manufactured by Amazon.ca
Bolton, ON